PICTURE PERFECT

For My friend Ellen,
Lisbeth

Love,
Misty Erwin

Picture Perfect

Misty Erwin

iUniverse, Inc.
Bloomington

Picture Perfect

iUniverse books may be ordered through booksellers or by contacting:

iUniverse
1663 Liberty Drive
Bloomington, IN 47403
www.iuniverse.com
1-800-Authors (1-800-288-4677)

ISBN: 978-1-4620-5041-3 (sc)
ISBN: 978-1-4620-5042-0 (ebk)

Printed in the United States of America

iUniverse rev. date: 09/15/2011

Prologue

So I waited. I waited until the temperature of the air dropped and I shivered. I waited until the light diminished and I couldn't see my own hand trembling. I waited when I heard a steady knock on the door. Even when they called my name, I waited.

Some people still ask me why I didn't answer. The answer is that I don't know. I was unable to respond, I guess. The smell of smoke burned my lungs and the sound of the sirens lured me into myself. I was as quiet as a mouse. Just as she asked me to be. I was a good little girl.

Chapter 1

Ashley

Ashley hurried down Main Street in her high heels and navy business suit. The clip-clop of her shoes reminded her of a horse when it trotted. This thought made her laugh out loud. As if thinking people shouldn't laugh out loud in public, an elderly lady slowed her pace to peer suspiciously up at her. It wasn't that people shouldn't laugh out loud; they just shouldn't do it in public. These days any sort of nonsense was viewed as psychotic. Just being happy seemed to attract a crowd. This thought also made Ashley laugh. "Oh well," she thought. "Let them be miserable. Today is my day! I will sing and laugh if I want to."

Ashley flipped her light blonde hair back over her shoulder and felt the slight breeze cool her neck. She loved her little town this season of the year. The shopkeepers swept off their doorways every morning, and people visited each other in the evenings. If anyone else noticed how happy she seemed on this day, no one commented on it. She waved a hello to three people she knew and continued on down the street.

She crossed over the street to Chris' Hair Salon. If anyone could understand Ashley's elation they would be found in here. "You who! Anybody here?" she shouted. "In back," a sing songy voice replied. "Mom! Stop being so old fashioned. All the girls will be there and Mrs. Chambers will be chaperoning the whole night! Aunt Ashley, please tell your sister that she is being unreasonable and that I am old enough to spend the night away from my mommy. I am twelve years old for goodness sake!" Ashley was smart enough to hide the smile that tried to fight its way to her face. She also knew better than to get in the middle of another argument between her sister and her niece. When matters of the pre-teen heart were at the forefront of the discussion she had no idea what advice to give. "Thank goodness Katie is only five years old," she told herself.

"Ashley, don't you dare!" Chris laughed with a sparkle in her eye. Christine Dosser looked nothing like her sister but they both had the same sarcastic sense of humor. She owned the only hair salon in town. "I think you should be able to do exactly what you want to do Carley. I think you are old enough to vote, drink and get married. As a matter of fact, you seem old enough to be able to pay your own bills, live in your own house and also to buy your own car."

Getting no help from her aunt, Carley turned on her heel and flipped her hair. The sigh she gave seemed to suggest that she wouldn't expect any less from her aunt. Everyone knew that the two sisters were loyal to a fault and after the door slammed they cracked up. "Guess that will teach her to ask my opinion," Ashley said. "Oh to be young and carefree. How was your day?"

"Well, let's see. Started off right away with old Mrs. Calvert. Imagine blue hair. Blue! She had the nerve to look offended when I snickered and asked her who her butcher was. Seems her granddaughter is here for a visit and wanted to try out a new color on her granny. Never let a seventeen year old experiment with your hair. Mrs. Calvert acted like it was my fault her hair was ruined. Had to either hack it off or turn it purple. Wasn't much of a choice. I think she looked pretty punky in violet. Oh and let's see. Drew came home from school after having made the decision that he needed to have a Mohawk. He said that all the kids have one. He is the only boy in school who has normal hair, can you imagine? Since I have the only salon in town and cut all the kid's hair, he couldn't argue that one. Now he and Carley are mad at me and I haven't even gotten home yet. Daniel has to work late again. I forgot to lay out the ground beef for supper. That just about sums it up. What about you?"

Upon turning around Chris looked more closely at Ashley. "Have you heard a single word I have said? Ashley! Why are you smiling?" Ashley kicked off her shoes, threw off her jacket and unbuttoned the top two buttons of her blouse. "I just met the most perfect man," she sighed.

"Well that's an oxymoron if I have ever heard one," Chris said. "Who in the world did you meet on a regular day in Clarkston? I haven't heard of any tall, dark or handsome man moving to our little neck of the woods. And believe me, if they did I would have heard by now. Seems like everybody in town plays matchmaker to poor Ashley. Twenty seven years old with a daughter and no husband. How shameful."

"Well, he didn't move to town. He was only passing through. Imagine the destiny that played a part in our chance meeting. There I was eating a regular lunch at Henry's when he came in. I immediately noticed him like he was a magnet or something. He walked right up and asked me out."

At this development Chris' maternal instinct kicked in. She had been protecting Ashley for about as long as she could remember. Even though she was only three years older than her sister, she had taken on the role of mother after their parents had been killed in a horrible car accident when Ashley was only four. "And you told him no, of course. You told him that ladies do not go out with strangers, right?"

Ashley rolled her eyes heavenward and sighed. "Oh my gosh, you are an eighty year old woman in a thirty year old body. Well, not exactly. I told him of course I would go out with him. I would have probably married him right then and there. I can't believe I did something like that. I mean, I don't even know where he is from! But Sis, you would not believe how nice and respectful he is. He opened the door for me and everything. Who ever heard of that kind of chivalry in this century?"

"What door? Where did you go with this stranger?"

"We walked over to Olson's Lake for a few minutes. I feel like we have known each other forever. Hey will you stop interrogating me for just a minute and let me boast? It's not every day that I get excited about a man. Not everyone marries her high school sweetheart and lives happily ever after, like you did. For heaven's sake, I dated Brad for three years before we got married and look how that turned out. The only good thing that came out of that was my wonderful daughter. Speaking of which, I'd better be going. Sandra needs to leave early tonight for her Bingo game. See ya soon, Sis!"

Ashley grabbed her jacket and shoes in one hand and just as quickly as she breezed in, she hurried out again. She didn't turn to see the worried look she knew was on her sister's face. Life was good and she was taking advantage of it.

Chapter 2

Ashley

Before her eyes opened Ashley knew something was wrong. There was a feeling in the air that could only be described as heavy and ominous. Normally she wasn't a person prone to such fantastic experiences. She wouldn't describe herself as whimsical or paranoid. As a matter of fact, she could not ever remember feeling a sensation such as this. When she placed her hand to her chest she was surprised to feel how hard her heart was beating and she didn't really know what had awakened her.

"Katie!" she shouted out into the darkness.

Immediately, she jumped out of bed. Not pausing to turn on the lights she stumbled into the hallway that led down to Katie's room. The ballerina night-light cast a dim glow on the slightly opened doorway of her daughter's bedroom. She burst through the doorway and felt blindly for the light switch.

"Katie?" she said again with alarm.

"Mommy?" a scared, sleepy, little voice asked. "What's the matter? Did you have a bad dream?"

"Katie." she whispered. "I'm sorry. I didn't mean to scare you. I was just checking on you. Everything is okay."

"Here Mommy. You can hold my doggie. He will take care of you. Whenever I am scared, I always hold him. I don't need him now. I am a big girl. You can lie with me, too". The little girl patted the mattress. Ashley stared down at her sleep tussled little angel. Her auburn curls trailed down her back as she rubbed her fists against her eyes. Had there ever been a more precious sight? Did all mothers feel this way about their little ones? Her heart hurt to even think that something could happen to her.

"Thank you honey, I will. I would love to sleep with you. Doggie will make me feel all better. I'll stay here with you. Go on back to sleep, little one. Back to your dreams now."

Comforted by her words, Katie quickly fell back into a deep sleep. Ashley, however, wasn't that lucky. When she closed her eyes, she could still feel the car start to slide sideways uncontrollably, and heard a woman's scream-the most bloody curdling cry imaginable. She knew that even if she covered her ears to escape the sound, it wouldn't work. The sound and feeling of her and her parent's car leaving the pavement and beginning to flip was ingrained in her soul. Ashley covered her eyes with one hand and rubbed Katie's hair with the other. She had never felt her responsibility so strongly. She curled up around her little daughter and said a prayer of thanks. The smell of her Elmo shampoo and her fresh pajamas slowly calmed her down. She forced herself to take regular breaths and to relax. Everything was okay, just like she had promised. She must have just had a nightmare after all. She had been having these anxiety attacks for years now. She must learn to accept her past as her past and let it go. But where to start? It was just at times like this, in the middle of the night, that sometimes the weight of the world came crashing down and her defenses abandoned her.

Katie

In the beginning she didn't even realize what she was doing. Her feet seemed to move of their own accord. Stopping to pick up a bright orange leaf, she knelt on the cool soft grass at the edge of her yard. With only a little fear she found herself peering down into the lake water. Her reflection bounced back to reveal that her butterfly barrette had slipped almost all the way out of her hair. She bent closer to see herself better. That is when the leaf slipped out of her hand and landed in the water about a foot away below the old wooden dock. Maybe if she stretched really hard she could just reach it.

She wanted to show Mommy the leaf. They were making a book of leaves to show Sandra. Mommy said Sandra needed special things to make her happy. Her husband was in heaven and that made her sad. Mommy said it was a special place, but Katie knew that she just said that to make her feel better. Every time anyone mentioned Heaven, they were always crying and sad. Maybe it was a time-out place. Time-out always made her sad and cry too. Maybe she would be brave and just ask Mom.

Katie knew one thing for sure. She didn't want Sandra to be sad. She had taken care of her for so long she couldn't even remember when she didn't. She had watched her when her mom was at work since Katie was little. That must have been years! Sandra helped her make paper dolls and she even played tea party with her. Most big people didn't like to sit on the floor but Sandra did. She always grunted and acted like she couldn't get up off the floor on her own and this made Katie laugh. Sandra also made special pancakes shaped like Mickey Mouse.

With a start, Katie heard her name being called. She hurried up the dock and ran into the trees that led into the yard. Mommy didn't want Katie to go down to the lake. She said it was dangerous. Katie didn't know why because it was so pretty there. Sometimes, she went to see the fish and once she saw a frog. Of course, Sandra or Mommy was with her then. Mommy had said not to go there by herself, ever ever ever. Too late, she realized she had disobeyed her mommy. If she found out where Katie had been she would be very angry and Katie would be in big trouble.

Quickly she skipped to the swing set and yelled, "Here I am, Mom!"

"Katie, there you are. I looked all over for you. Time to come in for dinner sweetie". And she slipped her hand into Mommy's larger one and the pretty orange leaf was forgotten floating in the lake.

Ashley

Later that night, Ashley found herself double checking the locks on the doors. For the third time she looked to be sure the security lights were working. What in the world am I doing? This is a nice neighborhood. We have never heard of any type of break-in around here. I must be tired, she thought. Living alone for so long had taken its toll on her. Sometimes she wished for her sister's life. A caring husband who came home every night and kissed her. Someone to count on. Someone who she could trust to love Katie just as much as she did and share the responsibility.

Oh well, so much for dreaming. Time for reality. She had work early in the morning and it would be Monday, too. Mondays at a bank were always stressful. So much paperwork to catch up on. And she had her date with Mr. Wonderful to look forward to on Friday night. She couldn't suppress a smile at the thought of seeing him again.

The week wound its way down like expected. Monday night Parent's meeting at Katie's school. Tuesday dinner with their neighbors the McNealy's. Wednesday night church and Thursday a fashion show at home trying to decide what she would wear on her date. "Good grief, girl. You'd think this was your senior prom the way you are acting. A man gives you a compliment and suddenly you act like you are in love!"

"Shut up. I seem to remember your first date with your hubby. You got completely ready in that new denim outfit and then dropped your Coke in your lap because you were shaking so hard."

"Well, I was also seventeen years old! You aren't a child anymore, Ashley. Frankly, I am a little worried about you. We just don't know this guy and he might be a serial killer. Where are you going?" Chris said.

"Just out to eat to Olivia's. I will be back to get Katie by nine o'clock. I told him I would have to keep it short because Katie would need to get into bed." With a straight face, Ashley couldn't resist, "If I am not back by then, call the authorities." She had to duck to avoid the playful slap she knew was coming from her sister.

Friday night turned out clear and cool. Ashley was putting the finishing touches on her makeup when she heard the doorbell. Let him wait for me, she thought. They say that a woman shouldn't look too anxious. At least that is what all the magazines said. She didn't know how that might pertain to someone real. After a few minutes she rushed to answer the door. Little did she know that Katie had already answered the door and let him into the living room. By the time Ashley entered the room, they were engrossed in a floor puzzle shaped like Barney. "Yeah, sometimes on Saturday mornings, I get up early just to watch the old episodes of Barney. Don't tell anybody though. People might laugh at me."

"That would be ugly if they did. My mommy said not to make fun of people. She said that we should treat everyone the way we want to be treated. It's the Golden Rule. Besides, why would they laugh at you for watching Barney? I watch it all the time and nobody makes fun of me. All the kids at school do too. I like the last song the best."

"Me too, as a matter of—." The latter part of his sentence was cut off as Kevin realized that Ashley was listening at the door. "Caught me red-handed," he said, putting his hands up in the air with an ill-concealed smirk. "I like Barney. Go tell the world." She was so impressed that she forgot to chastise Katie for opening the door. Ashley burst out laughing. It had been so long since she had seen a man playing with Katie that it had momentarily caught her off guard. Who was this fellow?

"Sorry I got here a little early. Didn't take as long to drive up as I thought it would. Nice home you have here. And may I say that your daughter is delightful."

"Well, thank you sir. I like her myself. She is so sweet that she reminds me of me." she laughed.

"This should be an interesting night" Kevin said.

Six hours later, Ashley found herself sitting in the front porch swing with Kevin. Katie had long since been tucked into bed and their conversation hadn't slowed yet. There seemed to be so much to talk about. Kevin told her how he had grown up in Missouri with six brothers and five sisters. He had sixteen nieces and nephews. At Ashley's shocked expression, he only laughed. "What? You think I act like an only child or something?"

"No, not at all," she laughed. "I just can't imagine all those people around. Are you close to them?"

A shadow passed over Kevin's face. "Well, I was. My mom passed away two years ago and left her estate to me. This started a family feud that eventually ran me out of the state. I decided to come south and see what life would be like at a little slower pace." He seemed to be thoughtful for a minute before changing the subject. "Have you ever noticed that old house at the end of Holder Lane?"

Startled, Ashley hesitated before exclaiming, "Of course I know it. I have dreams about that place. I once ran away from home and ended up in that old house. I have always imagined what it might have been like years ago when it was first built. Of course it has gotten more and more run down over the years. Hard to see the beauty now. Why do you ask?"

"Well I just noticed it the other day when I was driving by. It got me to thinking . . . Can you imagine the beauty it would be if completely refinished? Modern appliances, refinished hardwood floors. If someone took the time and energy to truly love that house, bit by bit."

The moonlight shining on his upturned face revealed a passion so intense it took her breath away. What would it be like to have those eyes turned to you in such a way? She felt her heartbeat quicken and her pulse race. Quickly changing the subject, she said "Well, I'd better go check on Katie. She can be a sneaky rascal. Sometimes she finds her way down the hallway and watches TV over my shoulder way after she should have been asleep. I hope CSI isn't too intense for five year olds." She knew that she was rambling on and on but couldn't seem to stop.

"I'll take that as a hint to head on home. I have an hour drive anyway. I really enjoyed tonight, Ashley. I hope we can do it again sometime soon."

"Me too. I had a wonderful evening."

When his headlights backed out of the driveway, she sighed.

For the next two weeks Ashley found her thoughts returning to Kevin more and more often. They talked nightly on the phone. She wondered what was wrong with him. No good man was single at their age. There had to be some flaw that was unnoticeable until you really got to know him. Maybe he was a party-goer. Maybe he kept a string of women in various towns across the nation. Maybe he was really an axe murderer.

"What are you thinking about?" Chris said.

They were chopping vegetables for dinner, hoping they could enjoy a few more dinners on the deck before the weather turned too cool. The children were running around the yard playing chase and hide and seek. Of course, Carley stopped smiling the second any adult looked at her. She was too old to be enjoying games with children. At this the two sisters exchanged a knowing grin.

"Oh just the usual." Ashley replied.

"In other words, Kevin. Kevin this, Kevin that, Kevin this, Kevin . . ." smiled Chris.

They had been out twice more since the first date and each time was more and more fun. They were a natural match. They seemed to believe in the same morals and felt the same way about basic human nature. The first time his hand touched hers it was a like a shock went through them both. She looked up at his dark blonde wavy hair and blue eyes and smiled in amazement. She had finally found her soul mate. Just as she was wondering if she was overreacting, Kevin gazed down at her upturned face and whispered, "Wow! My angel."

"Earth to Ashley. That is enough carrots and zucchini to feed five entire families. Did you invite the neighborhood and forget to tell me?"

Sheepishly, Ashley smiled at her sister. "Sorry Chris. I guess I'm just bad company tonight. Will you give me an honest answer if I ask you a hard question?"

"You know I will."

"Do you think I messed up with Brad? Should I have tried harder? Was it my fault?"

"No I absolutely do not, Sis. Yes, I did dearly love him. But all respect for him was lost when he decided to give up his rights to Katie. I don't care how things were between you and him, a father who would rather have money than his daughter is hopeless in my opinion. Any doubt I may have had disappeared that day. He must have been putting on an act all along. And man, did we all fall for it. Look, Ash, I know I never tell you this but I am so proud of you. You are doing a wonderful job of raising Katie by yourself. You have proven yourself time and again. She is a wonderful little girl who knows about love and home, and you shouldn't worry about her not having a father in the picture."

At this unexpected revelation, Ashley found tears in her eyes. She did always worry about Katie. She thought she was doing pretty good, but how would she cope without her father and how would Ashley explain to her how her father decided to move away and have no contact with her in exchange for not having to pay child support? What would that do to a child? Luckily, Katie hadn't asked too much yet. But in the next several years, she was bound to notice that she only had one parent and start asking questions.

"Enough of this sappy stuff. Let's go get the chicken off of the grill. The kids are starting to wind down," said Chris. Arm in arm, the sisters walked off the porch to assemble the crew for dinner.

Kevin

He slipped on a crew necked shirt and khaki pants. Brown loafers completed the outfit. Looking in the mirror he saw that his eyes seemed different somehow. Happy, he decided with a smile. The sad look he had grown so accustomed to was gone. In its place was a look of anticipation and joy. His lips couldn't keep from smiling. They had been right. Brad's ex was pretty and he was a stupid man for leaving her. And the kid. She was a cutie too. Stayed out of the way most of the time.

They were taking Katie along tonight. Ashley was so hung up on the kid it was bound to impress her if he acted like he wanted her to be around. Maybe he'd take them to the fair in Hampton. That seemed like something a family might do together and the sooner Ashley started thinking about them as a family the better.

Ashley

Fifteen more minutes, she thought. It had been five days since she last saw Kevin and it felt more like five years. Good grief you do act like a teenager, she chided herself. You'd think you had never seen a man before.

The fact was that she felt so at ease with him that it was like a sigh of relief to be with him. He took control of what they did and let her relax, something she wasn't used to, yet she needed. It came as a complete shock to her that she actually liked him being a little bit dominating. Probably it was a relief after years of making all of her own decisions.

Tonight they were taking Katie to the fair. Katie had been so excited she had hardly slept last night. "Uncle Kev" as she had taken to calling him was picking them up for dinner beforehand. Pizza, he had said. Katie's favorite meal.

From the top of the Ferris Wheel they could see all of the lights of Hampton. It was such a breathtaking view that Ashley felt herself tear up. Katie squealed with delight. At first Ashley had balked at the idea of taking Katie on the ride.

"Why are you scared?" Kevin had asked.

"I don't know. She seems too little. She might get scared and want off and then what would we do?" she asked while glancing at the tattooed man who controlled the ride.

"Darling, she might love it and ask to do it again and again. Please. You have to let her live. She will be fine. I will be there to help you and her both," he said with a soft smile.

And, in the end, of course he was right. How had he known she would love it? She was her mother and hadn't known. If not for Kevin, Katie would probably have gone into adulthood without riding a single ride.

Left up to Ashley, Katie would be coddled and smothered in her mom's arms. Could he see the love in her eyes, she wondered. "I am falling in love with a man whom I have only known for four weeks. Heaven help me."

Chapter 3

Katie

The black shadow in the corner of the room looked like a monster. If she looked really close she could see its teeth. It was a dragon. Tommy had told her all about dragons last week at school. He said they lived in the corners of your room at night and came out to eat you when you were asleep. At the time, she had laughed at him. But now she could see that he had been exactly right. Any minute now she would feel its breath on her neck and it would eat her up. "Mom!" she screamed.

"Mom!" a little louder this time. She couldn't get up and run because it might catch her. Katie pulled the covers up over her head and started to cry. Softly at first and then louder and louder. Where was Mommy? Did the dragon get her, too? It was so hot under these covers, but no way was she coming out. "Mommy? Where are you?"

Then she heard her mom's footsteps running down the hallway. "Katie? Honey? Are you ok? What's wrong?"

Bright light filled the room. Katie jumped up off the bed and lunged at her mother. She looked over her shoulder at the corner of the room and saw nothing. The dragon was gone.

"Mom, there was a dragon over there. It was going to eat me!" she cried.

Her mom's arms felt so good around her. She let herself be wrapped up and lifted. She buried her face in her chest and cried. Sometimes she felt silly being held since she was almost grown up but right now she needed to smell the familiar scent of jasmine that always surrounded her mother.

"Honey, don't be scared. I am here. It was just a shadow. See? Look over there. The lamp was just casting its shadow on your dresser, and your imagination got away with you. Everything is fine."

Fearfully, Katie did as she had asked. Nothing unusual. Her Barbie's lined the shelves. Barbie's pink jeep was upturned on the carpet next to the bed. Two pairs of shoes. Nothing. How would anybody ever believe her if he disappeared when people came in? "Where did it go?" she asked in amazement.

"There are no such things as dragons. They only exist on TV. Who told you there were?" Mom inquired.

"Tommy said they live in your room and eat you. He was right. I saw it! It had glowing eyes and long sharp teeth!"

"Sounds like Tommy has been watching too much TV. Let's go get in my bed and go back to sleep, sweetie. I have to work tomorrow and you have to go to school. Please believe me when I tell you that there is no dragon. Monsters only live on TV. Ok?" Mom said softly.

Katie tried hard to believe her. She knew that her mom would never lie to her, but it was hard to deny something you had seen with your own eyes.

Chris

Seems like it's been forever since I saw my sister, she thought. She spends every weekend with Kevin. He seemed like a nice enough fellow. They had met briefly when Ashley and Kevin dropped Katie off last night. Certainly attractive. Carley had made goo goo eyes at him as soon as he walked in the door. At this she laughed. When Chris had walked into Carley's room unannounced later on last night, she had seen Carley drawing Kevin's name on her notebook. Carley's first crush. Ah, those were the days.

She walked through the living room picking up toys and clothes, mentally making notes about what they needed at the grocery store. She jumped when her cell phone vibrated in her pocket. "Hi Honey! What's up?" she asked.

"Again?"

"Ok, well, be careful. I'll be waiting up for you. Why? That late? You are spending too much time on the road. You only ate with us two nights last week. I know, I know. Please try to be here tomorrow for Carley's band concert. Ok. Love you too. Bye."

Another night without Daniel. She really needed him tonight too. He was her rock. Sometimes just being with him was all she needed to unwind. Seeing Ashley all in love made her realize just how far off the mark her marriage had been lately. With her working and him starting the new job they just didn't have the time together that they used to enjoy. It was taking its toll on her and the kids. Carley was more and more belligerent. Drew had been acting up at school and at home. She would just have to sit down with Daniel and talk to him about it this weekend. Maybe they could take a vacation together. Somewhere nice and secluded. No cell phone service. Seemed like every time Daniel actually was home, he had the phone glued to his ear.

Ashley

It had been a very long day. Ashley rubbed her eyes as if to wipe away the memory. Two customers had been in to argue about their statements. The president of the bank had asked her to put out a memo at 4:45. And to make matters worse, Katie had fallen after school on the swing set at home and broken her arm. Sandra had called her in a state of panic to tell her that she was on her way to the hospital with Katie.

Now it was 7:00 p.m. and they had just gotten home from the hospital. Sandra had finally been convinced that it wasn't her fault that Katie had fallen. Poor lady always took such good care of little Katie. Unfortunately, Katie was a bit head strong and had convinced Sandra that it would be ok to practice a new move one of her classmates had taught her. Seemed simple: Hang upside down by her legs on the jungle gym and then let go with her hands. Place her hands on the ground and then drop her feet to the ground. A Cherry Drop, they called it. Well, that move had definitely been practiced for the very last time. Ashley sighed. She knew Katie well enough to know that she would probably sneak and try that move until she had it perfected no matter what Ashley said.

The medication the doctor had given Katie had made her groggy. Ashley was trying to decide whether to put Katie in bed or try to feed her something when the doorbell rang.

"Who in the world?" she thought. She peeked out the window to see who it was and was shocked to see Kevin standing on the other side of the door shuffling his feet and wringing his hands.

"What are you doing here?" she asked as soon as the door was open.

"Well, I was expecting a hello, honey, good to see ya, but I guess that greeting will have to do," he laughed. "But why are you here? I just wasn't expecting you. Is something wrong?"

"Not at all. Just wanted to check on the little one. I heard she had broken her arm. Is she ok? I went to the hospital, but they said she had already been released. They told me about her arm. I'll bet she is in a lot of pain. Is the medicine helping that at all?"

Stunned, Ashley stood speechless at the door. "How did you know about this?" she asked in wonder.

"Well, I do have a telephone," he said. "Not that you used it to call me. You act like I shouldn't be here. I'll go. I'm sorry to bother you."

"No wait, Kevin" she called out to him. He turned halfway down the walkway. "I was just shocked that's all. I didn't know anybody would call you. I am just a mess. Katie was so scared and crying. I just got in and was debating about dinner. Please come in. Excuse my manners," she apologized and went to embrace him.

Hours later, she was lying in bed thinking about the day. Oh, please let tomorrow be better she thought. My poor baby. But the thought that kept arising was Kevin. Finally unable to sleep she decided to call him. I'll just make sure he made it home okay she told herself.

After two rings he answered his cell phone. "What's up, babe? You ok?" "Yes, Kevin. I'm fine. Just checking to be sure you got home ok."

"Oh, I'm fine. It's you I worry about. You and Katie living all alone up there. I feel the need to protect you. I'm sorry if I alarmed you tonight. I guess I overstepped my bounds by coming there and trying to help."

"No, not at all. Actually, it was nice to have someone here to help me with Katie for a change. I guess it is just taking me some time to get adjusted to it. I've spent so much time alone and all. Oh, I forgot to ask. How did you get the hospital to give you her information?"

"Oh that was easy." he answered with a chuckle. "I told the doctor I was her dad".

As the dark night sky started to lighten in the horizon, Ashley found herself sitting on the front porch drinking coffee. She had been unable to sleep last night. What was wrong with her? Hadn't she been so excited about Kevin? He was so perfect. What was bothering her about him? She guessed that she just wasn't used to him being there with her. She also didn't know who would have called him and told him about Katie but she felt that he would be offended if she asked. Oh, stop it, silly Ashley! Wasn't this just exactly the man she had been praying for all along?

Katie

She had found that if she tried really hard, she could write with her left hand. The letters looked somewhat crooked but at least she could do her homework. Sandra had helped her with her homework tonight and now she was really tired. All the kids at school thought Katie's cast was really cool. They took turns writing on it with Magic Markers. Joey had drawn an upside down heart. She traced the heart with her finger and thought about things.

She felt bad about falling and breaking her arm. Mommy had been so scared when she ran into the hospital room. So had Katie, but she had tried so hard to be brave. Even when the doctor had to touch it and push on it and it hurt so badly, she had tried.

Sandra had made her special chocolate chip cookies today. She had eaten three even though Mom had said only two. Right before she slipped off to sleep she thought about Kevin. She missed him. He always made her laugh, even when her arm was hurting. But, best of all, Mom was so happy when he was here. I wonder how it would feel to have him kiss her goodnight and tuck her in, she thought. Just like a daddy.

Ashley

She and Kevin had slipped into a sort of routine rather quickly. Even though a relatively short amount of time had passed since she first met him, she felt as though they had been friends for a long time. Since he lived so far away, she had suggested that he stay in the guest room on the weekends. "I bet the rumors are flying about town," she thought with a smile. They usually spent all weekend together and she hated to see him go on Sunday night.

She had gotten used to him being there on Friday nights with surprises up his sleeve. Sometimes he brought dinner ingredients and made her and Katie something delicious in her kitchen. Other times he took them out. By Monday morning she was already waiting for Friday again. He seemed to brighten her life in a way that she needed so desperately.

It was so easy to depend on him. He didn't seem to mind helping with bath and bedtime with Katie. He understood her need to be attentive to her daughter. Sometimes she just needed a minute to unwind after a hard week, and he knew that as well. He would take Katie for a short walk around the block and whisper to Ashley to go take a bubble bath or just enjoy a cool drink on the back deck. These precious minutes alone were so special to her. She couldn't believe that she actually trusted another person to help with Katie, except her sister and family of course. She was used to Chris helping with the daily chores that parenting demanded. Chris was always there to lend a hand with dinner, running errands, or relieving Sandra if Ashley had to work late.

Speaking of Chris, Ashley had noticed that she was quieter than usual this week. She would have to remember to ask her what was up. She heard a car in the driveway and slipped out of her reverie. Par for the course, Kevin arrived right on time tonight and true to his customary self, he had a remarkable surprise in store for them. In hand were two handkerchiefs.

"Ok ladies, tonight we will start with a little excursion. Please turn and face the opposite direction. I will attempt to tie these blindfolds comfortably yet securely."

Katie giggled. Kevin smiled. Ashley was so happy to have them all together that she really didn't care where they were all going. "A little adventure huh?" she asked.

"Yeah, I have something new to show you and I don't want to give it away before we get there, so turn around, woman, and let me tie you up."

She couldn't help but smile at the double meaning. When she met his eyes, she blushed. He leaned closer to her and quietly whispered into her ear, "Later." The passion she saw in his eyes matched hers and she couldn't take her eyes away from his.

With her heart skipping, she asked "So, Mr. Mysterious, where are you taking us today?"

"You'll see soon enough. I hope you girls don't get car sick."

Several minutes later, the car came to a stop. The crunch of gravel beneath the tires didn't give anything away. Kevin had made so many turns and changes in direction that Ashley had quickly lost her sense of direction as well. What was he up to? Like a child, Ashley giggled in anticipation. She stood a bit unsteadily and waited while she heard Kevin helping Katie out of the car, too. When they were all standing and waiting Kevin asked, "So, girls, who wants to guess where you are?" he asked.

"The zoo?" Katie questioned.

Everybody laughed at that one. Katie had been begging to go to the zoo for weeks now.

"Well, not quite. Maybe a hint will help. Ok, this is something I have dreamed of all my life."

With a wink, Ashley smiled. "Well, you already have me, Kevin. What more could you want?"

She heard him move to take her into his arms and she felt his breath on her upturned face. "Ashley, you must know how much I love you. You are all I have ever dreamed of and nothing that comes after this can ever be more special than you are to me."

At this revelation, Ashley held her breath. Had he really just told her that he loved her? She had been waiting for months for him to let her know how he felt. Still reeling from the moment, Ashley was momentarily speechless. She was no less shocked when Kevin whisked off the blindfold and standing in front of her was the dilapidated mansion on Holder Lane.

"A haunted house!" Katie shrieked.

"Not exactly a haunted house, honey. Only a beautiful home waiting to be discovered. And it's mine. Finalized today."

Ashley couldn't find her voice. Shocked was an understatement. "This is yours?" she asked in wonder. The object of her obsession now belonged to Kevin? He hadn't mentioned the house since that time right in the beginning of their relationship, so she had forgotten that he was interested in it. Regardless, she didn't realize that he was serious enough to actually follow through and purchase it. Nobody had ever seemed to want this deserted place. It had been vacant for as long as she could remember. Except for the occasional stray cat and sometimes teenagers needing a place to drink, nobody ever even looked at it. But now that she was standing in the overgrown driveway she had a chance to really look at the details.

"Kevin Landers, if you are kidding me I will kill you right now." Ashley threatened as she spun to face him.

"Cross my heart, this house belongs to me. You are standing in my driveway. And I want you to just visualize the beauty that she beholds. All the original woodwork is still in good shape. The stained glass windows are worth almost as much as I paid for the whole place. Look past the weeds and the cobwebs and the broken railings. Picture the majestic scene she will be when I get finished with her. And, I want to share all of this with you. Both of you. Not just the house, but all that goes with it. This will unfortunately require some work, as you can see, but also the years of happiness I hope to have within these walls. I want this to be our home. I want to share my life with you. Will you accept my proposal and become my wife?"

Ashley was so dumbstruck that she couldn't even breathe. Surely she had just imagined this. Had he just asked her to marry him? She shook her head as if to clear it. Throughout this exchange, Katie had been strangely silent. Now she piped up, "Kevin do you want us to live with you in this old house and you can be my Daddy?" Ashley was mortified. What if he hadn't meant that?

"Katie!" she shouted.

"Don't yell at the girl, Ashley. At least she has something to say. Here I am pouring out my heart to the girl of my dreams and you just stand there and stare at me like I have two heads." he laughed out loud.

Startled out of her stupor, Ashley replied, "Kevin, you are the most intriguing person I have ever known. You wine and dine me, charm my daughter, and then out of the blue you announce your desire to have us become a family. We've only known you for a few months but I feel as if you are a part of us."

"Well, is that a yes or a no?" Kevin teased.

"Katie, what do you say? Would you mind if Kevin and Mommy got married and we all lived together?" Ashley asked after bending down to eye level with Katie.

"Would I have to call him Daddy?" Katie whispered.
"Not unless you wanted to," Ashley said.
"Well, okay, if he will clean up his house. This place is creepy." At that Ashley and Kevin met in an embrace and both of them cried tears of joy. It felt so right to be in his arms. When they felt a little nudge, they accepted Katie into the middle of the huddle. Ashley was laughing and crying at the same time. "Katie do you want to go explore?" she asked.

After Katie had disappeared around the side of the house, she looked up into Kevin's face. "Oh my goodness, I can't believe this is happening. Are we engaged or am I just dreaming?"
"I was just thinking the same thing. How could I get so lucky as to find you and Katie? This is the best day of my life."

With that, hand in hand, they went to find Katie. They found her crawling under the rose trellis on her hands and knees. "Katie get up off your arm. You will get dirt inside that cast and we will never get it out!" she exclaimed.

"Mom! I heard something under here. Something moved and I think it's a puppy."

"Let me see, honey. There are bound to be spiders and ants and all sorts of things little girls are suppose to be scared of. My sisters wouldn't have been caught dead crawling around under there when we were kids. Say, I think you might be right. Come on out little one. Hey, it is a puppy. A very dirty, scared, and hungry one, but a puppy, never the less." With this he produced a furry bundle from underneath the rubble.

"Oh you poor thing! Where in the world did you come from?" Ashley cooed.

She immediately took the puppy in her arms unmindful of the mess he made of her pink sweater. She started trying to pick the leaves and dirt and sticks from its brown and white fur. Well, mostly brown right now, but she figured that light color was supposed to be white. "I think you are a she. And I also think you may have the prettiest blue eyes I've ever seen. On a doggie." Ashley added at Kevin's hurt look and pouting lips.

"Give her to me, Mom. I found her and that means she is mine. I love her and will take care of her and feed her and water her. Let's go give her a bath!" Katie squealed. Without a second glance, she took off back around the house towards the car. "Well, looks like we have ourselves a dog." Kevin said. "Hope you're not allergic." "Thank goodness, no. She has been asking for a dog for ages but I was trying to wait until she was old enough to help take care of it. We had one when she was tiny but he died after only a couple of days. Seems like this dog picked us instead of the other way around. I hope the little thing isn't sick, too. She would be devastated."

Kevin smiled at the emotion on Ashley's face. "You, my dear, are a sucker. You are already in love with that stray. Well, that's alright. That's what I love about you. Taking in anybody who needs you. That's what you did to me, too." She playfully slapped him on the arm and then leaned over for a kiss. "Don't be silly. You are the one who zeroed in on me at Henrys that day." With a laugh, they began to walk back to check on the two new friends. They found Katie sitting on the front porch steps holding the dog and talking quietly to her. "And my mom is the best. She will help me take care of you. We'll wash your hair and brush it and then maybe Kevin will go get you some food. I'll bet you are starving. All you had to eat under that rose bush was leaves and dirt." She heard Ashley and Kevin approaching. "Mom, hurry and let's go. We need to get Rosie home. She said she was tired and hungry."

Katie was already halfway to the car when both adults burst out laughing. "Ok so I guess we have a dog named Rosie in the house and she is already requiring work and making demands. Typical female." Kevin said while dodging another blow from his new fiancé.

This day couldn't be any better, Ashley thought to herself.

Katie

She couldn't believe that she had a puppy. For years she had been asking her mom for one. Now, as she sat on her bed stroking Rosie, she was so happy! Katie wondered where the little dog had come from. Surely she had a mommy and a daddy somewhere. Well at least a mom. Katie didn't have a daddy, so maybe Rosie didn't either. But Katie bet that somewhere out there the mommy dog was missing Rosie.

"Don't worry, mommy dog. I will take very good care of your baby," she whispered out her open window into the darkness.

The next morning Katie was surprised that Rosie was still asleep. She hadn't cried or barked or anything. She had simply curled up beside Katie on the bed and went fast asleep. She must have been tired. "Time to get up Rosie. Today I have to go to school and you will have to be here alone for a while. But I will be back as soon as I can. Then Sandra, you and I will play outside in the leaves. Come on, sleepy head. Let's go get some breakfast."

They both scrambled down the hallway to see Mom talking on the phone. "Okay, see you tonight!" Mom said to whoever she was talking to. She hung up the phone and turned around. "Well aren't you both the cutest things I've ever seen?" she said. "Katie, tonight we are going to Aunt Chris' for dinner."

"Can Rosie go, too, Mom? I've already promised her I was going to play in the yard with her," Katie asked.

"Sure, I'm sure that will be fine. The dog will just be another surprise for Aunt Chris tonight," her mom said. Katie looked at her mother. When did she get to be so easy going? Kevin sure had changed her mom. She was so happy since Kevin had started coming around and Katie sure hoped that he kept his promises.

Kevin

Today was the day. Demolition day. He had a whole crew of people lined up to help with certain parts of the restoration of his new house, but most of it he would complete himself. One of the things he enjoyed most about construction was, oddly enough, destruction. He loved taking the old and making it new again. There was nothing like looking at a blank slate and envisioning the beauty it could become. Today, they would be removing the old garbage that years of teenager's parties had left in the house. There seemed to be hundreds of pounds of aluminum cans in the kitchen floor alone. Ashley had joked that he could sell the aluminum for enough money to completely refinish the house.

Today, he would also begin removing the old roof. That was a definite priority because there were several leaks he had discovered up in the attic. Years of squirrels and bats occupancy had left nests up there too. Better to get that out of there before Ashley saw it. He planned to make their bedroom up there and if she saw the mess, he would have a hard time selling that idea to her. She was one tough woman but he had yet to run across one who liked bats, rats and the like.

"Ok Kev, time to quit thinking and start doing," he said aloud. He loved the way an unoccupied house seemed to absorb words. He liked to imagine that if the house could talk it would have an amazing story. Think of all these walls had seen!

"When I agreed to marry you I didn't know you were prone to talking to yourself." Kevin jumped and turned around to face her. Laughing he caught her up in his arms and spun her around. "I guess I failed to mention that small fact." he said.

She begged for him to stop. "What are you doing here? I thought you were going to work today?" he asked. With her head still spinning she replied, "I took the day off. Actually I called in sick. First time in my life I have ever called in sick just to have fun."

"Fun? You think this is going to be fun? Well, you are going to love it when you see the rotten wood in the living room then," Kevin exclaimed. "What are you waiting for? Daylight is wasting, my lady. Grab that roll of garbage bags and get to work."

Two hours later they met again. They both burst out laughing when they saw the condition of the other's skin and clothes. Both were covered in dust and grime. Ashley's eyes were swollen and running tears that streaked down her dirty face. "I can't believe I am facing dust allergies for you." she sniffed. "You poor baby. But just imagine the joy we are going to have within these walls. And just wait until you see where your new bedroom is going to be." he said.

She followed him up the two flights of stairs to the attic. "You must be joking. There is no way I am sleeping in this creepy tiny space." she said. Her voice seemed to be swallowed up in the darkness. "Just you wait and hold judgment until you see my handiwork," he bragged. "Just be careful up here until I get the floor replaced. A person could easily fall through these old rotten joists. And please warn Katie, too. I don't want her up here until later on." "Ok, I will, honey. Thank you for being so caring. I'm sure this will be beautiful when you get finished with it. But for now, I think I will just stay downstairs. Surprise me." She seemed to glance around in distain and disbelief. "Now come on and see your new kitchen." He followed her down the stairs to see the progress she had made. It had seriously taken her eight large trash bags to pick up all the litter. He couldn't help but laugh when he saw all the bags lined up next to the door. "Kevin, if you think this is funny I am going to leave!" And she playfully stamped her foot like a child would. Kevin smiled and covered his mouth with his dirty hand. "No, no. It just looks like Santa's house must look on Christmas Eve. You did a wonderful job, sweetheart. I didn't know there were hardwood floors in here." He bent down and pretended to be amazed.

"Well, I swear. I never thought I would see the day that old Kevin Landers would be down on his hands and knees in front of a woman," a strange voice said from behind them both. Ashley turned and stared at the stranger. Her hand had automatically gone up to cover a scream.

"Ritchie! You old man! You did show up after all. Come on in and meet my fiancé." Kevin greeted the man with a thump on the back.

"Hello, ma'am. I am pleased to meet ya. I am also surprised to find that old Kev here talked you into speaking to him, much less marrying him. What did he do, pay ya?" he laughed the loudest, most raspy laugh she had ever heard.

Ashley was so shocked that she forgot to reply. Kevin came up to her and stage whispered, "It's ok honey. Ritchie might be a little rough around the edges but he has been my best friend since childhood."

"Oh, I'm sorry, Ritchie. I didn't mean to seem rude. I just didn't know you were there. I am happy to meet you." She couldn't keep her eyes from the long ragged scar that ran the length of this face. And try as she might, she couldn't help but notice the clothes he were wearing were old and out of date. They were at least two sized too big for him

"Well, don't just stand there staring. Let's get this house restored. Kevin here tells me you want to move in right in after the wedding and that means we only have two months to get this old place fixed up."

Ashley looked up at Kevin surprised. Oh great, two minutes and already Ritchie was running his big mouth. He would have to remember to reiterate the rules to him later on.

He left Ritchie working on removing the old wood from the kitchen floor. "I only told him that so he would have mercy on me and help. We can get married whenever you want to, honey. I know we haven't even discussed a date yet. But, I for one, can't see much reason to wait around. When were you thinking?" he asked with a little trepidation.

"I don't know. I just sort of figured that we would get married next summer. I haven't even told my sister and her family yet. I was going over there tonight to tell them. Do you want to come with me? It would be so wonderful to be together when we broke the news."

One thing he didn't like was big families. And big family gatherings where people looked at him.

He tried furiously to think of a reason to decline, but couldn't seem to come up with a reason fast enough. She took his hesitation as shyness. "Oh, Kevin, you don't have to be scared of them. They are the most wonderful people you will ever meet. And they are going to be so happy for us. We'll just plan to leave around five and go get cleaned up. I told Chris I would be there around six for dinner. I can hardly wait."

Neither can I, Kevin thought to himself.

Chris

Whatever could be keeping Ashley? Chris had everything almost ready for dinner. She was about to call and check on Ashley when she heard the sound of gravel crunching in the driveway. Popping the rolls in the oven, she went to the door to greet Ash and Katie while wiping her hands on a dish towel. "Better late than nev—" the last of the sentence hung in the air between the three newcomers and Chris. "Oh, excuse me, Kevin. I didn't know you were here. Come on in!" she called out, not a little awkwardly.

Ashley smiled when Katie dashed up the stairs to find her cousins. Kevin moved into the den to talk with Daniel. They had met only briefly before so Ashley hurried in to ease the transition. She found them already engaged in a discussion about the pros and cons of hiring subcontractors and doing the work yourself. Not wanting to break up their conversation, she quietly moved back into the kitchen to help Chris with setting the table.

Chris was laying out the silverware when she arrived. "Well, you could have mentioned that Mr. Wonderful was coming. I would have fixed something special tonight. All I planned was salad, spaghetti and bread," she said as she laid down a fork a little harder than necessary.

"Oh don't worry, silly, He loves spaghetti. He isn't royalty, Chris, calm down." Ashley teased, but she was a little surprised at the anger she felt in her sister.

"Well, you wouldn't know it by the way you act. You have all but forgotten about us. I haven't even seen you since last week. You used to come over three or four nights a week. Now I have to call and schedule a date just to check on you. Did you forget Carley's chorus concert Wednesday? She waited on you to show up. It seems to me that you have gotten too serious about Kevin too fast." Chris lowered her voice and moved closer to Ashley. "Who is he anyway? Have you even asked him where he came from?"

A high, piercing, beeping sound saved Ashley from answering. The men ran into the kitchen to investigate. The kids entered at about the same time. All at once the kitchen was bulging with people and the beeping kept on. "The bread!" Chris screamed. She turned and opened the oven door and black smoke billowed out. Daniel fanned the screaming smoke alarm with the broom. Finally the smoke was cleared from the air and the evil alarm went back to quiet. Chris and Ashley met eyes over the chaos and Chris sent an unspoken apology with her eyes. Ashley turned her back and went to Kevin's side. Chris was embarrassed about her outburst. Ashley had done nothing to deserve that tongue thrashing. She didn't know why she couldn't seem to be friendly with Kevin. She usually was very outgoing and talkative but when he was around she clammed up. Suddenly she realized that tears were coursing down her cheeks and she turned and fled the kitchen in shame. On the back deck she sat down on the steps and started pulling the dead petals off of a daffodil. She knew Ashley was there even before she spoke. The air changed when the two sisters were together. She tried to wipe the tears away without being seen but of course Ashley knew. She felt the pressure of her little sister's hand on her shoulder as she lowered herself to sit beside her. A tissue was offered and accepted.

Why didn't Ashley get mad? She had never gotten angry at Chris. Even when Chris had tried to boss her around when they were teenagers, Ashley had played the part of the obedient little sister and acquiesced. Never once in all their lives had Ashley had enough and shouted at Chris. Never once had she accused her of being overbearing. Somehow, that made it worse and she started to cry in earnest.

"Stop crying. You are ruining your makeup and the king is here for his dinner." Ashley joked.

"Shut up, Ash. Don't make jokes. I am an idiot. I don't know what in the world happened to me. Kevin seems like a wonderful man. I have no reason to dislike him except that I am jealous of your time with him. That is so silly of me. My goodness, we aren't kids anymore. Please believe me when I say that I am extremely sorry, sis."

"Apology accepted. I hope that you will come to know Kevin the way that I do. You will realize how genuine and loving he is. Please just give him a chance to prove himself. Now let's go eat. I am starving." With that Ashley turned to go inside. A tiny bark caused her to turn back again.

Both women looked down into the grass to see Rosie waiting patiently for someone to notice her. "Oh, well so much for the surprise. This here is Rosier. We had her in a box beside the car. Wanted to show her as a surprise but maybe she saw that you needed a friend."

"Oh my goodness. Where did you get her?" Chris exclaimed between sniffles. She had the dog raised up under her chin and was kissing her soft brown and white fur.

Before Ashley could answer, someone spotted the puppy from inside. All of a sudden there was a flurry of bodies rushing outside to meet the new addition. Chris looked up to thank Ashley for her understanding, but her sister had already gone back inside.

Ashley

Ashley had been so excited about sharing her news with her family when they first got here. After the outburst from Chris she knew how awkward she felt about Kevin and she really wanted to wait. Maybe give it a few more weeks and invite Kevin to a few more dinners before she sprang the upcoming wedding on her sister. But one look at Kevin's face over the centerpiece and she couldn't seem to come up with an excuse. His eyes were alight with anticipation. His blue eyes seemed even bluer than before with the candlelight. The blond in his hair seemed to glow. "Oh my goodness. He looks like a Greek god," she thought to herself. She was truly caught between wanting to share in his happiness and wanting to be a buffer for her sister.

In the end she knew that she couldn't let Kevin down. After all, she wasn't a kid anymore. She had been married to Brad and had Katie. She owned her own house and paid her own car payment. Had Chris been there for her over the years, yes. Had Chris stayed up all night with her when Katie had colic, yes. Had she stood by Ashley through all of life's ups and downs? Yes. But now Ashley had found the perfect man for her. He was a perfect match. Now she must stand on her own two feet and branch out.

"Well, now that dinner is over, Kevin and I have an announcement to make." She reached across the table to grasp his hand. She was shocked to feel that his palm was just as sweaty as hers. This made her a little less nervous. They were in this together and she could survive anything with him by her side. As if he heard her thoughts, he got up and came over to her side of the table to stand behind her. He placed both hands on her shoulders and before she could say any more, he said "Daniel and Chris I want to thank you for the lovely dinner. Thank you for opening your home to me. I know that I just came into your lives and we really have only started to get to know each other, but I was hoping that we could be friends for years to come. You see, I love Ashley. I love her so much that it breaks my heart to see her worried about disappointing you. I have asked Ashley to be my wife and she has accepted my proposal."

He didn't even slow down when Chris gave a startled gasp or when Carley whooped for joy. "I know how much she loves all of you. You have all been such a part of her life. I only ask that you will allow me into that close circle. I promise that you won't be sorry." In the silence that followed, Ashley had time to look around the table. Unaware of the magnitude of the moment, Katie was reaching under the table and feeding Rosie a piece of her bread. Drew was spinning his fork around and around his plate. Carley was beaming at Kevin with true love in her eyes. Daniel jumped to his feet and clasped hands with Kevin, then came around to hug her. "So happy for you both. So happy. I hope you will love each other as Chris and I do," he said.

Finally, Ashley ventured to look over at Chris. To her surprise, she found her smiling and crying. Tears once again washed down her face. Unnoticed, the tears dropped onto the green tablecloth. Dark green splotches appeared and left marks on the cotton. "Ashley," was all she said. Then she was up and running around the table to clasp her little sister in her arms. Ashley was so shocked that she couldn't even speak. Tears made her throat close up and speech would have been wasted anyway. They didn't even need words. She felt the love Chris had for her in the way that Chris held her. After a few minutes, Chris recovered enough to release Ashley and go to Kevin. "Kevin, I am so happy for you both. Please take care of her and Katie."

"I intend to make them so happy that they never even have time for worry. Oh, and I almost forgot about another part of our future. Ashley, do you want to tell them where we will live?" he asked with a wink. "Live? Please don't tell me you will be moving?" Chris asked faintly.

"Yes, sweet sister. But not like you think. This part of the story just brought home the fact that Kevin was heaven sent. Where have I dreamed of living since we were little girls? Do you remember when I ran away from home when I was eight? Where did you find me?" Ashley asked.

"Well, I found you sleeping on the steps of that old house on Holder Lane, but I can hardly see you living there!"

"Maybe not now, but in a couple of months you will be able to. I bought the place. Ashley and I spent the day cleaning up some of the inside of the place. We plan to completely remodel it and live out the rest of our lives there."

Kevin

Chris was looking at Kevin as if he were some kind of angel. Or was that suspicion in her eyes? There was certainly a lot going on behind those green eyes of hers. He would have to watch her.

Katie

Everything had changed. Since she got Rosie she didn't need Mommy to be with her all the time. Now she had a friend who played fetch, tug-of-war and chase. She loved her puppy so much. Rosie was the best doggie in the whole world. She slept on the corner of her bed and kept watch so that Katie could rest without worrying about monsters. Katie had decided that she would do anything for her. When Rosie had an accident in the house, Katie would hurry and clean it up before Mom saw what had happened. Mom acted irritated when the dog did that. Katie was afraid that Mom might make them find a new home for Rosie. Maybe people didn't think kids knew bad stuff, but Katie did. She had seen a show on TV. about animals without homes. She would do whatever to make sure that she and Rosie were together. With a laugh, Katie ducked one of Rosie's wet kisses.

Mom even acted different lately. Sometimes, when Katie was talking to her she just sat there and stared out into space. Then she would nod and smile like she was listening but Katie knew that she wasn't. But, Katie didn't mind. She knew about love. She had also seen a show on TV. about that. Love makes people happy. Mommy loved Kevin. And Kevin loved Mommy. That was o.k. with Katie, as long as everybody loved Rosie.

Ashley

Today was going to be fun. Finally, Saturday had arrived so that she could be off work and go see how much progress Kevin had made on the house. She hadn't been there since Monday when she had taken the day off work. He had been quietly elusive on the phone each night. He was working late and hadn't even come by the house to see her. Unconsciously, she frowned. Man, she missed him! He said he had a surprise he was working on and she couldn't wait. Katie was so excited! They were going to the store downtown to pick out colors for her room this evening. Ashley was envisioning a little window seat and pastel walls. Flowers on the curtains, and a doll house. Chris had always told her that she lived in a fantasy land. Maybe she did.

The light traffic in Clarkston on this Saturday morning slid by unnoticed by Ashley. She was just anxious to see Kev and the work he had done. Katie was talking softly to Rosie in the backseat and Ashley couldn't resist a smile. It was so wonderful to have someone who loved Katie as much as she did.

When they pulled up into the driveway Ashley held her breath. All of the windows had been removed from their frames. The roof was brand new and looked out of place on the old flaking white paint. Most of the wraparound porch was gone except for several new support beams. It's becoming our home, she thought.

Katie jumped out of the car almost before it came to a complete stop. "Uncle Kevin! Uncle Kevin! We're here!" she yelled at the top of her voice.

Ashley heard the clomp of boots on the stairs and Kevin appeared, like a vision. He looked rugged in this flannel shirt with the sleeves rolled up and his old worn blue jeans. He had stubble on his face that made him seem so sexy.

Kevin caught Katie up in a hug and swung her around. "Want to go see something awesome?" he asked.

He reached out for Ashley's hand and kissed her on the mouth with so much passion that it took her breath away. "Wait until you see this!" he said. While she was still reeling from the heat of the kiss he took off up the stairs. Katie was close on his heels with Rosie right behind them. Ashley lightly touched her fingertips to her lips wishing that she could cast this moment in her mind forever. Everything was so perfect and the anticipation of the future held her in its grips.

Kevin

This was so perfect. He ran up the stairs with the whole crew at his heels. When they were all in the room that was to be Katie's, he held up a hand to quiet Katie's questions. "Without further delay, I will present my housewarming gift to my future daughter." From the closet area he withdrew a white post. With the same air as someone presenting an Olympic medal he placed it into Katie's awaiting arms. "What is it?" she asked with some disappointment. "Well, it is part of an antique canopy bed," he said.

At Ashley's shocked expression, he smiled. "You are giving me a bed post?" Katie asked. Both of the adults laughed at Katie's puzzled expression. "Just you wait and see what this will look like when it is finished," Kevin said. At Ashley's frown, Katie hesitantly said, "Thank you, Uncle Kevin, for the wonderful post."

"You're welcome, Katie. Maybe I am out of practice dealing with five year old girls." he laughed.

Losing interest in the gift, Katie began to play fetch with Rosie with an old piece of wood she found on the floor. But, Kevin wasn't finished with surprises yet. He quietly took Ashley's hand and led her to a small room off to the left of Katie's that they planned to be a study. He took her face in his hands and leaned in for a soft kiss. Her smile made all the work worth the extra effort. Slowly he lowered his left hand and produced a small box from his pocket. "What do you have?" she asked.

"Open it and see. I found these in a box up in the attic." Ashley hesitantly opened the box. Inside, wrapped in a thin piece of tissue, were two rings. Both were made of white gold and studded all the way around with diamonds. Just looking at the rings made Ashley's eyes water. "Who do they belong to?" she asked in awe. "I don't know, but I bought the house and they were concealed up in the rafters of the attic, so now they belong to me and you. What do you say that we wear them as wedding bands? Go ahead and try yours on. I already did and mine fits perfectly."

Ashley gingerly lifted up the narrow band and placed it around her finger. "Perfect," she whispered. "How is that possible?" He loved the way she looked up at him in amazement. "And just wait until you see the engraving on the inside," Kevin said. She looked closely and saw what he had seen earlier—FOREVER. One simple word that meant so much. When Ashley looked up into Kevin's eyes she saw a love mirrored there that she had only previously read about in books.

Kevin was impressed at his ability to read this woman. She was so sentimental and loved all things antique. He had known that she would treasure the idea of old love renewed. How had he been so brilliant?

Chris

It wouldn't really hurt anything to check him out, would it? That was the only way she was going to be able to completely trust Kevin Landers. And there on the desk was the tool she needed to do it. But each time she started to begin, she felt guilty and stopped. It seemed like the computer glared at her all day. When she started down the hallway with a basket of laundry, she looked over her shoulder at the computer. When she got in from taking the cat to the vet and laid the keys on the desk, she also stared at the computer.

Wasn't anyone else even a little bit worried? Didn't seem like it. Everybody just took him at his word and fell completely in love with him. Why didn't she? Well, because Ashley loved him, and he had just come from nowhere-that's why. Any fool could see that Ashley was completely snowed by the man. She wouldn't know she was in danger if he stabbed her with a knife. Oh gosh! That did it!

She ran to the computer and turned it on before she could think about what she was doing. Nobody would know. That was unless she found out that he was dangerous. Oh, shut up you moron! Of course, his story would check out. Simply type in his name. Or, so-called name. She couldn't help but laugh at herself. Who would have thought she would be so suspicious? She waited while Google sorted out all the Kevin Landers in the world. She tapped her fingers on the desk while she waited. Gosh, Daniel hated it when she did that. Just thinking about him made her smile. If he could see her now he would have the laugh of the year.

Kevin Landers—entrepreneur in Chicago
Kevin Landers—pet store owner in Haiti
Kevin Landers—dress maker in New York

The list kept on and on. Where was it Ashley had said he was from? Up north somewhere like Montana or Michigan? How was she supposed to figure this out without all the information she needed? She couldn't just ask him for his previous address or social security number. She didn't

47

even know where he was staying now. She doubted that Ashley did either. Sighing in exasperation, she shut the computer off. She would just have to keep her eyes and ears open for a sign that Mr. Landers had something to hide. For now, she didn't know what else to do.

Carley

If the girls at school could see Kevin they would die. He was the cutest guy Carley had ever seen. And last night she was sure that he had brushed up against her on purpose. She didn't know if she would ever get a boyfriend or not. It was only last year that she had noticed boys at all. Billy Joe at school was currently bugging her to death. Kids! Seems like the boys at school were so stupid and immature. Not smooth and sure of himself like Kevin. When he smiled at her, she melted. How did one get old enough to handle herself the way that Ashley did when she was around him? She was always so pretty and confident. She could be stern with Katie at the same time that she was teasing Kevin about his lack of patience. She could look at Chris and act like she was listening to her when Carley knew that she was actually listening to Kevin and Dad talking. Carley could tell that Ashley didn't want to miss a single thing that her guy said.

Carley decided that she was going to start trying to act like Ashley. She would try an older hairstyle and maybe go shopping with Ashley and let her pick out some clothes for her. She would study the way she smiled and the way she walked. Yes, she would be Ashley in training. This thought made her smile all the way to fourth period.

Mrs. Martin was going on and on about fractions. Who was going to use any of this stuff in real life? How often did Mom need to know how to divide one sixteenth by four twelfths? She should be doing something meaningful, like art class. Now that is something that got her attention. She dreamed of being a famous artist one day. Of course, she didn't tell anybody this dream. Mom thought she should try something academic like being a scientist or neurosurgeon. Dad always talked to her about the day she would become an attorney. Whenever she mentioned doing something creative, everybody just acted like she was telling them a joke.

"CARLEY DOSSER! Ten seconds to answer the question or detention for you! I am tired of your daydreaming and less than excellent school work." Too late Carley realized that the entire class was looking at her. Joshua was snickering into his hand. Her best friend Mary was trying to get her attention. She was holding up three fingers on her left hand, which was hidden from the teacher.

"Why of course the answer is three, Mrs. Martin." Carley said sweetly
.

"I don't know how you pulled that one off but be sure that I will be watching you, Carley. Your mother was an excellent student and I wouldn't want you to fall by the wayside." One bad thing about growing up in a small town like Clarkston was that everybody knew everybody else. And Mrs. Martin knew more than most. She had taught school for forty six years and knew everybody's family tree back to the Great Depression.

Immediately after school Carley found Mary waiting by the door. "Carley, that was a close one. I almost passed out!" Mary had a knack for being a little over dramatic. That was one of the things that drew Carley to her the most. Another was that Mary was so innocent and played by the rules. She made Carley feel like a rebel. Mary looked at her like she was some kind of hero when she did something not quite normal. Sometimes she liked to tell Mary that she was going to become a nun if she didn't start acting like a normal twelve year old. This always got them to laughing and giggling but Carley secretly wondered about the truth in that. Oh well, she would just have to wait and see how life turned out for the both of them.

Ashley

The past six weeks had flown by. Each day was an adventure. She was always ready to get up and face the day ahead. After work almost every day she picked up Katie and sometimes Sandra to go see the house. It was absolutely amazing how much work he had accomplished. All the floors had been completely refinished. New windows were installed. The special stained glass had been professionally cleaned and reinstalled. All the walls had a new coat of paint and the trim had been painted as well. All the rotten wood had been replaced in a way that was not noticeable at all. The original chandeliers had been rewired with the rest of the house and hung majestically from the vaulted ceilings. All new stainless steel appliances finished off the state of the art kitchen. Viewed from the front door entrance, the stairway and banisters were breathtaking.

Today was the first day that Sandra had been to the house in several weeks. She audibly gasped when she walked into the foyer. Every conceivable convenience had been thought about and Kevin had spared no expense. Yet, whenever Ashley asked him about money he always brushed her off.

"Ashley, how in the world did you find this man? Your world is about to change." she said reverently.

"Looks like the house is almost complete. When are you guys getting hitched?"

At this Ashley paused to look at Sandra. This woman who had been married for forty years was rushing her into marriage?

"How long did you and Henry date before you got married?" she asked.
"Exactly six weeks, my dear. I knew the moment I saw that man that I would love him until our lives were over. Now that he is gone, I feel like half of me went with him." She paused to wipe a wayward tear from her eye. Then she put her arm around Ashley's shoulder and started walking towards the bright, clean kitchen. "Now, girl. One thing you must know is that a man loves good cooking. And with a kitchen like this, there is no reason not to know how to cook. As soon as you move in I am going to

give you lessons. I can't have you living under this beautiful roof and not using this kitchen."

"Yes, ma'am," Ashley said. "Speaking of the wonder man, where is he?" She went through the bottom level of the house calling his name. When she finished there she went up the stairs. There she found Katie playing in her new room. Rosie had found an old shoe and was busy trying to kill it.

"Kevin!" she shouted. "Mom, he is outside. Don't you see him?" Katie pointed out the window to the garden below. Ashley went over to the window and peered out. Just as Katie had said, there he was. Was there anything this man didn't know how to do? All the brambles and thorns and fallen trees had been removed from the yard. In its place was a garden that would be fit for a queen. He had put in a pathway out of flagstones that led to the gazebo that was currently being built by three men that Ashley didn't know. Along the right side of the pathway Ritchie was helping Kevin install a koi pond, complete with a waterfall. Ashley ran down the stairs and burst out the back door. All eyes turned to her and all the men stopped working to see who had interrupted their work. Someone whistled through his teeth.

Embarrassed, Ashley trotted over to Kevin, "Hey, honey. I had no idea that you were going to start on the outside today. This is absolutely beautiful!" She turned around and around, exploring the wonderful world he had created.

Standing up straight and glancing over his shoulder, Kevin began to walk towards her. When he was next to her he grabbed her by the shoulder and spun her around. Ashley was stunned by the look of anger on his face and her smile quickly was replaced by a gasp. He grasped her wrist tightly and pulled her along behind him as he angrily strode away. She had no choice but to follow him or risk being bruised. She followed him to the side of the house out of earshot of the others. He bent so close to her ear and spoke so low that she had to strain to understand his words. "Do not ever come in the presence of my men wearing clothes like that. You look like a whore. Understood?" Like a scared little girl, she simply nodded. "I won't have my wife being viewed as a slut and talked about behind my back. If any of those men so much as speak to you, I will kill him."

With that, he turned on his heel and headed off the way they had come.

Unable to stand any longer, Ashley sank down onto an overturned barrel. She raised her hand to wipe her brow and was not surprised to see that a purple bruise was already starting on her wrist. What in the world had just happened? She needed to think. She needed to get out of here. Quickly, she ran into the front yard and into the house. She found Sandra exploring the home. "Sandra, can you watch Katie for me? I need to make a quick trip into town." After being assured that Sandra could stay, Ashley ran outside and cranked the engine. She was about to back out of the driveway when there was a knock on the window. She screamed. Kevin was standing there gesturing for her to roll down the window. With resignation she did as asked.

"Where are you off to sweetheart? I thought we were going to have dinner together tonight," he asked as if nothing had happened.

Shocked, she was unable to answer. Never in her life had she been treated so harshly by another. And now he was acting normal. She peered up into his eyes and searched for the answer. Instead of anger, she found only gentleness and kindness. The Kevin she was used to was back. This thought scared her more than the physical assault. Before she could speak, he said, "Look, honey. I am sorry about what happened back there. I just had a moment of jealousy, that's all. I don't like it when another man looks at you. Can you forgive me? I swear I will never lose control like that again." Then he leaned down and kissed her. She saw that there were tears in his eyes.

Kevin

He would definitely have to work on his temper. One thing that he couldn't afford to do was to rough her up again. She wasn't used to being handled like that. Shoot, she probably had never even been spanked when she was a kid. The look in her eyes had scared him there for a minute. She had looked like a scared rabbit trying to outsmart the fox. This thought brought on a wave of laughter. Outsmart! Yeah, right. Dream on, little lady. She had no idea who she was dealing with.

Katie

She loved her new room. Well, what was finished so far anyway. She loved the lilac color she and Mom had decided on. Kevin was trying to put together her new canopy bed now. She was helping him by handing him the tools he needed. He was teaching her the names of all these tools. Phillip's head, flat head, pliers, etc. He said that he would even let her use the drill in a minute. Kevin didn't treat her like a baby. Mom had said it was too dangerous for her, so Kevin had given her something to do downstairs.

"Let's get this done while Mommy is away, huh?" It was a little secret. She loved being part of something grown up. Mom was always scared of everything.

When the final pieces were assembled, Kevin shook Katie's hand. "Great work, there, partner." Now she could lie in her bed and pretend to be a princess. She didn't have a mattress yet, so she used her imagination. "Kevin?" she called when he turned to leave. "Yeah, partner?" he asked. "When can I start calling you Daddy?"

Sandra

Almost suppertime and still those three were up there fiddling with the bathroom tile. Seemed to never get tired of this fixing up stuff. Oh, well, she thought. If my Henry had wanted to stay up all night doing tile she supposed she would have done it too. She just couldn't imagine how Ashley had gotten so lucky to find Kevin. He seemed like a genuine gentleman. He helped Sandra with the door and never forgot to thank her for helping with Katie. He always complimented her on her cooking, too. She was glad to help the happy couple. These days, young people had a hard enough time without having to worry about dinner. So much to think about and do. She personally hoped they would go ahead and get married soon. That wonderful Mr. Kevin. Couldn't afford to let him go. Too many women in the world would sell their souls to find someone like him.

Ashley

Ashley was having trouble concentrating. The red or the gold? Which color to use in the kitchen? One was bold and made a statement. One was strong and comforting. "Ashley?"

"Yeah, Sis. Come on into the kitchen. Thank goodness you're here. I am just about to make the final decision on the paint color and I sure could use your opinion." Chris came into the room and looked around.

"Wow," she uttered.

"Yeah, wow. Can you believe this is going to be mine? And do you know that it is just exactly as I always dreamed it would be? Down to the bay window and the wraparound porch. Everything about the house is perfect."

"Perfect. Yes, that is a good word, darling." Kevin said as he entered the room. But instead of looking at the house he was busy looking at his fiancé. Mischievously he wagged his eyebrows up and down. Ashley playfully threw a dishtowel at him. Dodging the towel, he ran into the living room to continue with his work.

"He seems so good to you, Ashley. Is he really always that nice?"

For a brief moment Ashley considered confiding in Chris about that one episode to see what she would make of it. Who knows? Maybe all men were prone to spurts of rage and jealously like that? Brad hadn't ever shown physical anger, but he was usually too wrapped up in himself to notice her anyway. She wondered if Daniel had ever done anything like that. Especially in the beginning of their relationship when things were not yet finalized. Of course, Kevin was under a lot of stress with the house and the wedding and all. She had probably just over reacted. As usual. Goodness knows that people were always telling her that she was like that. Maybe this time they were right.

Katie

Mommy and Kevin were downstairs arguing. She tried to be quiet and listen to what they were saying. She was supposed to be in her new room playing but she had snuck out into the hallway and was barely able to make out their words. "But it just doesn't seem right to not even invite any of your family. I want to at least start out our marriage with the hope of reconciliation. What could have happened so bad that you don't even want your brothers and sisters knowing about your marriage? I am sure that if you will just make the first step, some of them will be willing to at least talk to you. I can't imagine anything Chris could do to make me completely forget about her."

"I said no, Ashley. Stop trying to be a peacemaker. I am finished with that bunch of people."

"But, sweetheart-"

"No buts. I said no. Final answer. No way, no how, I am speaking to any of them again. Please don't put me through this."

Katie heard a shuffle of clothing that told her that Mom had moved closer to Kevin. They made some muffled sounds but Katie couldn't understand any of what they said. Who were they talking about? She didn't know Kevin had any family. She had never seen any of them before. Actually she had never even wondered where his family was. Oh well, she and Mommy would just be his family now.

Chris

Chris paused in her job for a minute to get a glass of water. She was in charge of installing the hardware on the kitchen cabinets. Boring work, but useful, at least. The brushed antique knobs Ashley and Kevin had chosen were perfect for this house. She was leaning up against the cabinet looking around when Kevin appeared from the side porch door. "Oh Chris. Wow, you are making nice progress in here. Where are those kids of yours today?"

"Carley had band practice and Drew is at football practice. Nothing that child likes better than playing some type of sport. He is playing quarterback you know. Mr. Hot Stuff." They both laughed at that.

"What about Carley? Is she happy playing the clarinet? I mean, does she really want to be doing the whole band thing?" he asked.

Chris thought this was a strange question coming from someone who had only known them for a few months but she tried to find the right answer. "Yeah, she likes it. Better than the tuba." She laughed. But when he didn't too, she knew that this wasn't the answer he was waiting on.

"No, I mean does she like playing musical instruments or do you like for her to do it?" She peered at him quizzically. "Well of course she likes it. Why do you ask? Did she say something to you or Ashley?" Chris wondered.

"No, I just wondered, that's all. She seems a little distant. I just remember being a teenager and no one understanding what made me tick," he said with a sad smile. This made Chris a little angry and she couldn't help but feel insulted. Who did he think he was? How could he possibly know what Carley wanted? She turned her back and began to work on the knobs again in earnest.

"Look, Chris. I know that we sort of got off on the wrong foot, but I just wanted to say that I love Ashley. That means that I love all of you too because you are a part of her. I am sorry if I seem a little sharp and too up front. That is just the way I am. If I think it, I usually say it. Don't take me the wrong way. Please try to like me, even if just for Ashley's sake."

"Oh, don't be silly, Kevin. I like you just fine," she stammered. After he had turned and left she finally breathed a sigh of relief. What was it about him that set her off? She would have sworn that earlier today when she was talking to Ashley she had seen a shadow cross her face when they were talking about Kevin. Just a flicker of doubt, but enough that Chris had noticed. Of course, she hadn't brought it up because she didn't want to do anything to upset Ashley. Now she wondered if maybe she should be asking some really tough questions, whether it caused conflict or not.

Kevin

One more week and he should have the house ready. Only a few more finishing touches here and there. Whenever he drove up into the yard, he would have to say that he was impressed. This place was off of a postcard. Picture perfect. This thought made him laugh out loud. Picture perfect, yes you could say that again.

Ashley

One thing that Ashley couldn't understand was Kevin's adamant decision not to invite his family to the wedding. They had decided to go ahead and have a small ceremony on November 5. That was only two weeks away. She didn't feel right being the only one who would have family there to witness the celebration, especially since he had such a huge family. Surely out of all those people somebody would have made the effort to come. How could money tear a family apart?

After their parents were killed, Chris and Ashley were sent to live with their Aunt Anita. She was their mother's sister and had been everything to them both. Unfortunately, Aunt Anita had passed away six years ago. She had been sixty five when they went to live with her and she had never been married. She was a quiet lady with simple tastes and not much interest in material things. What little money and possessions she had left were divided equally between the sisters and that was that. No family feud. Of course, she supposed that it would be a different story if a lot of money was on the line. She wouldn't know. Her family had always been working blue collar people, with nothing to fight over after a death. She wondered if millions of dollars were on the line, if things might have been different. She tried to imagine quarreling with Chris and then turning her back and running across the nation. Couldn't be done. But then, she and Chris had been through hell together. She supposed that made a difference. Since she knew next to nothing about Kevin's family she couldn't make the comparison. Hopefully, over time he would open up and talk to her about his family. Sometimes it was hard to verbalize traumatic events. But she felt quite sure that she could help him deal with this. She was so good at helping people. With this thought, she finally fell asleep.

Sandra

One more week and the big wedding would be here. She was so excited to see Ashley happy. She had been so devastated when that ordeal with Brad had happened. They had all had him pegged totally wrong. He had truly seemed like a nice guy, always helping out with whatever needed to be done. And building things? That man was a genius at construction. However, he had obviously fooled all of them. Turned out to be a hoax. As soon as news of that baby girl came along, he changed. And before she knew it, he was gone. Completely gone. Signed away his rights to Katie and everything.

Oh, well. No use crying over spilled milk, her mother had always said. Time marches on. Now things would be better for Ashley and Katie. Now they had Kevin. And best of all, he had already told Sandra that they would be keeping her on to help with Katie. That had been a relief, especially after he had whispered that he was going to make Ashley quit work. That was a good idea in her book. When she and her honey had been married she had never worked outside the home. Her job had been to keep the house and make him happy. Oh, how she had enjoyed doing just that. She had been afraid that the young couple may not need her anymore. That thought had scared her. Why, Katie was a part of her too. She had practically helped raise the child. Just thinking about her curls and mischievous smile made Sandra laugh out loud.

Ashley

Well, another day at work. She had to hurry if she wanted to be on time. She was running a little late today because Katie couldn't seem to decide which shirt she wanted to wear. Ashley had all but screamed at her to get her to hurry up. There hadn't been time for a time-out this morning. Then when they finally got to school she realized that she hadn't signed the permission slip for Katie to go on the field trip. She had dug through her Dora backpack and finally found it crumpled on the bottom. The cars behind her in the drop off line had honked their impatience.

She hated to leave Katie after a morning battle. She loved that little devil so much. Already she was ready to go home to see her and apologize for shouting at her. Tonight they would lay out her clothes for tomorrow. A little planning would hopefully help to avoid that chaos. Things had been hectic lately with all the work at the house and getting home late every night and that probably had a lot to do with the short tempers.

With a sigh she rushed into the office and turned on her computer. She hadn't even had time to stop by the employee lounge for coffee. Hopefully, the day would get better. No way could it be any worse.

It was after six when she arrived home. Home. This was the last week she and Katie would live alone. There were boxes stacked up all over the house. "Katie! Sandra!" she yelled. They must be in the backyard. Quickly she opened the back door and walked outside. She inhaled a deep breath and tried to relax. Work had been just as exhausting as the morning had started out. Maybe tonight she would treat them to dinner out. Hot dogs and onion rings and maybe even an ice cream sundae. She doubted if she could even find her pots and pans to cook with anyway.

She caught a glimpse of movement out of the corner of her eye. Sandra and Katie were sitting on the dock with their feet hanging down in the water. Didn't Sandra know that the water was probably too cold for that now? She started down to the lake, removing her shoes as she went. The cold earth beneath her feet felt so good. Dusk was falling. She would just give Sandra a piece of her mind. Katie would catch her death out here.

Moments later, they were all laughing at the little fish nibbling on their toes. Ashley could not remember the last time she had taken the time to just sit down and laugh out loud. Lately she had spent all her time working on the house and planning the wedding and packing up her house to sell. It felt so good to just relax and enjoy the moment. She tilted her head up to gaze at the darkening sky. Already she could see the first stars coming out. She felt Katie reach for and grab her hand. Ashley looked down at her upturned face and smiled. She could only hope that they would always be this happy.

Kevin

What was taking her so long? Seven o'clock had long since came and gone. Usually she rushed here after work to see him. Stop being a jerk! Poor girl worked all day and came on home to help out with the construction, not to mention raising Katie and packing up the house. He should try to help her more. She had to be under a lot of stress right now.

Next week she would be his wife. He would make sure that she was happy and never wanted for anything again.

Headlights in the driveway broke up his reverie. He heard Katie's laugh before the door even opened. That child was a delight. She wasn't the brat he had expected her to be. When she had asked him if she could call him "Daddy", he had almost broken down. He didn't deserve all of this.

Ashley

Two chili cheese hot dogs and a large order of onion rings were just what she needed. Katie was finishing off her chocolate milkshake. Oh, chocolate this late? She would never get the child to bed. It was going to be hard to get her up in the morning since they usually didn't stay out this late. But, she just couldn't seem to hurry tonight. She wanted to savor every minute. Time was ticking, and she had so much planning to do for the wedding, plus the move. She had a meeting tomorrow with the real estate company to list her house on the market. She didn't expect much trouble selling. It was a beautiful place and had served her well. Lots of people were looking for something like it to get away from the noise and pollution of Atlanta.

Chris was helping her with the wedding arrangements. She and Kevin had decided to get married in the gazebo in the backyard of the new house. Even such a simple ceremony took a lot of planning. She wanted lots of flowers. After the wedding ceremony there would be a reception with light appetizers and a live band would play. She hoped for people to dance, laugh and have a relaxing time. She had decided to wear white. She had a child but she felt like she deserved to wear white to symbolize their new start in life together. Kevin was in complete agreement. Let them wonder, those nosy people. Of course, he was in agreement about just about everything. The only thing he was adamant about was her seeing their new bedroom in the attic of the new house. He absolutely would not allow her up there. It seemed like every time she went there he was up there beating and banging around. What could he possibly have to show her? She already knew how talented he was. Just look at the house and you knew to expect great things.

"Earth to Ashley. Penny for your thoughts." Kevin leaned into her and whispered. She was propped up on her elbows daydreaming again. "I was just envisioning our future. Oh, and I was wondering about our bedroom." She smiled. "You'll see it soon enough. No peeking!"

"I wouldn't dare," she answered. "Better get going. Got to go get cutie in bed and to sleep. School tomorrow."

"So when are you putting in your notice at work? Or have you already did it?" he startled her by asking.

She was momentarily so shocked she couldn't respond. "Why would I quit my job?" she asked, with a stupefied look on her face. He seemed just as shocked as she had. "Because you will be my wife, silly. Why would you need to work?"

"Kevin, we have never discussed my not working. I didn't know you wanted me to quit. I like my job and I want to contribute financially. I am used to having my own money to spend how I want to."

"Well, it's not like I'm destitute. I plan to support you and Katie and I wouldn't put a limit on your budget. As a matter of fact, spend away. Buy whatever you want, sweetheart. The world is yours," he laughed.

She wasn't impressed. The independent part of her personality took offense at his presumptions.

"Speaking of financial matters, just where did you get your money? Are you living on that inheritance from your mother you told me about? What kind of work do you normally do? I mean, before you moved here? I would feel a lot better if I knew a little bit of background information on you, Kev. I feel funny when people ask me a question I can't answer about you. I want to know all about you."

"Well, since you seem concerned that I am going to leave you high and dry, yes. I am using my inheritance. My mother left me a large sum of money. You don't really need to know how much, just know that you will be well off. You can easily quit work and do fun stuff and be home with Katie when she gets out of school. Do the things you have always wanted to do. And as far as answering questions from people, they don't need to know anything. It is none of their damned business." She was surprised at the indignant look on his face.

"Maybe not, Kevin, but people do talk. My friends want to know who I am marrying and who will be taking care of Katie."

"I am going to take care of you both. I plan to adopt her, with your permission, of course. I have already spoken to my attorney about it," he stated matter of factly.

"Are you serious? I didn't know you had even thought about that. Oh, Kevin, that is so selfless of you to want to take care of someone else's child."

He took her into his arms. "Well, pretty soon she will be mine. Just like you will, darling."

That night sleep eluded Ashley. How was it that all of her questions were never answered? She realized that she had left Kevin with no more answers than she had started with.

Chris

Tomorrow was the day. She had worked long hours arranging endless flowers and folding napkins. Ashley seemed to be floating on air. She sang and danced all the time she was working. The men had erected a huge outdoor tent over the reception area in the backyard. They had put up thousands of white lights and hung twenty wind chimes in the trees to play a peaceful tune during the celebration. Everyone was praying for a clear and cloudless evening.

Sandra was on children duty. She had them all in the front yard making little bouquets out of toile for the bird seed that the attendees would throw. The caterers were all taken care of. Kevin had already tipped them very well to be sure that they produced a feast no one would ever forget. Chris heard Daniel laughing out back and went to the door to see what they were doing. He and Kevin were leaned together talking in a low tone. At the same time, they both threw back their heads and laughed.

"Are you guys working or playing?" she teased, with her hands on her hips. At their guilty glances she wondered what in the world they had been talking about. She couldn't help but feel puzzled.

Daniel seemed a little more elusive lately than he had before. In the past they were best friends and told each other everything. More and more lately she felt lonely. He was on the road so much and she was stuck at home without him. His life seemed exciting. He was constantly meeting new people and going to see new places. His job as a pharmaceutical representative put him right there in the middle of all these things. She wondered if she seemed boring and ugly to him.

Kevin left Daniel's side and came to stand beside Chris. "Sis, I was wondering if you would do me a little favor?" he asked. She felt a little uncomfortable with his arm thrown around her shoulder as if they were longtime friends, but duty held her there. "Sure, what do you need?" she asked in return.

"Ashley deserves to get out tonight. For goodness sakes it's the night before her wedding. Isn't she supposed to go do something?" He gestured with both hands. From his pocket he pulled out a wad of money.

"Here, Chris. Take my beautiful bride for a massage, facial, fancy dinner and a night on the town. I have already talked to Sandra about watching all the kids tonight. She will spend the night at Ashley's house with all of them. You can plan to be home around ten o'clock in the morning all refreshed and ready to get prettied up for the wedding. Don't worry about anything else here. Just go get Ashley and you guys head on to Atlanta."

Chris was tempted to throw his money back in his face. "Arrogant asshole", she thought. She wasn't used to being told what to do, especially by the likes of him. The way he talked to her made her feel degraded and belittled. She drew in a deep breath and before she could ruin Ashley's wedding, she took the offered money and turned to leave.

"Chris, be sure you watch over my little lady. Don't worry. I'll be taking good care of your man." Was that a threat? She turned to see his eyes but he had already turned and was walking back into the yard, his laughter making his shoulder quake. With fire in her eyes, she dared Daniel to laugh.

She stormed up the stairs into the guest bedroom that she and Ashley had planned to use as a dressing room. Ashley was sitting on the floor looking at her wedding dress. Tears were coursing down her cheeks. "Ashley, what's wrong, sweetie?" She went to her sister's side and took her into her arms.

"Nothing, Sis. Absolutely nothing. I am just so happy. Did you know that Kevin already plans to adopt Katie? She will have a daddy like other kids. This is the happiest time of my life. I don't deserve this."

"Why of course you do, silly girl. You are a wonderful person and deserve great things. Nobody deserves as much happiness as you do. I am sure you will be happy. But for now, get up. I am under strict orders to whisk you away for the night. Your fiancée was quiet adamant about it all, too."

With this she pulled the wad of bills out of her pocket and let them fall on the carpet below. They both gasped when they realized that there were over two thousand dollars in all.

"Chris, what in the world will we do with all this money?" she asked in wonder. With resolution, she stood up and grabbed Ashley's hands in hers. She tugged her up next to her and said, "I don't know, but I am surely going to try to spend every last dollar before tomorrow morning. We'd better get started".

Katie

Tomorrow was the wedding. She had seen them on t.v. before. She was going to be the flower girl and she was very excited. She had a new dress to wear and it made her feel like a princess. Being the flower girl was a very important job. She stifled a yawn and tried to listen. Sandra was reading all the kids a bedtime story but Katie was having a hard time paying attention. Her thoughts kept returning to what had happened today. Every time she thought about it she almost started to cry. But she knew that crying would cause people to ask questions and she didn't want to talk about it. She pulled Rosie a little closer to her. Goodness she was growing so fast! She was as long as Katie. She felt so good when she snuggled with her. Rosie licked Katie's nose and made Katie giggle.

Maybe Kevin hadn't meant to kick Rosie. Probably he had just meant to scare her a little-teach her a lesson. Rosie had been playing under the ladder that Kevin was climbed up on. He dropped a tiny piece of wire and Rosie had playfully run and grabbed it and started to run off. Kevin had jumped down off the ladder and ran after her. Right before they went out of sight at the corner of the house, Katie ran after them. She saw Kevin reach the puppy and jerk the wire back. Katie had started to laugh at Rosie and call her name, but she saw Kevin kick Rosie in the side so hard that she had rolled over and over and yelped. Katie had been so scared she had hidden behind a stack of folding chairs. Kevin had been saying bad words and pointing at Rosie who was cowering on the ground. Finally, when Kevin went inside, Katie had ran over to Rosie and helped her up. There was a knot on her ribs where she had been kicked. She silently stroked her puppy and whispered to her to comfort her. Slowly Rosie had stopped shivering. It had taken Katie longer.

Katie wished her mom were here. Mom had promised that they would spent the whole night together since it would be their last one alone together; instead she had left with Aunt Chris. Katie wondered if Mom was already forgetting about her. She dearly loved Kevin, but tonight she was feeling a little scared.

Sandra

The big day was here. She would get the children up and dressed and head out to Chris' hair salon around ten o'clock. Chris was going to be fixing everybody's hair and that was bound to take a while. Sandra started the oil in the frying pan. She also started boiling water for potatoes. She would bring plenty of fried chicken and potato salad to keep everybody going today. It was the least she could do. The children had been so easy last night except little Katie was a little quieter than usual. Probably just nerves. Kids felt things like this. She knew that her life was about to change and that was bound to make her act a little different.

She remembered her wedding day. She had been so excited and scared. That seemed like so long ago now. All the kids were grown and had kids and grandchildren of their own. She was just glad that she had this family to work for and help. Old people needed to keep busy and the best way to stay young was to be with children. Maybe Ashley would have several more kids. That thought made her smile all the while she was making lunch.

Kevin

Kevin struggled to get out of bed. To say that he had partied all night would be an understatement. His head was pounding like a drum. His mouth felt like it was filled with cotton. Where was Daniel anyway? He glanced around the couch he was lying on and covered his eyes with his hands. Why were those curtains open? The sun felt like it was piercing his brain with a thousand needles. Oh gosh, he needed aspirin! Slowly he rose up on one elbow and looked around. From the photographs on the coffee table he gathered that he must be in Chris and Daniel's house. Carley and Drew smiled out at him without a care in the world.

"Daniel!" he shouted, then immediately hung his head in his hands. "Shut up, you drunken fool," was the reply he received.

Daniel laughed at him from the kitchen doorway. "Get your drunk self up and get some coffee. Your wedding is today and I am quite sure that Ashley will expect you to be there." He tossed Kevin four aspirin which he immediately swallowed dry.

"Wonder what the girls did last night?" Daniel said.

"Nothing as innocent as we did, I am sure," Kevin said sarcastically. He couldn't imagine Chris and Ashley going to see men strip or drinking themselves silly.

He was about to comment further when his cell phone rang in his pocket. Ashley was on the line. "Honey, hey! What are you up to?" she asked. Kevin had to hold the phone away from his ear to keep from screaming in pain. Why did she sound so loud and happy?

"What did you boys do last night?" she asked.

"Oh, you know. Just went out to get some wings and watched the game on t.v.. May have had one too many beer though," he said with a wink at Daniel. Daniel almost spit his coffee out when he heard that.

"Oh, you poor thing. Take some aspirin so you will feel better soon. We have a wedding to attend today! I am so excited! Chris and I went to the spa. I have never had a full body massage before. It was heaven. Then they put some kind of warm mud all over my body and—"

"Enough, woman. I can use my imagination for the rest. Don't tease and torture me!" he laughed, grimacing at the pain. "Hey honey, I will see you this afternoon, ok? I really need to go on over to the house and finish up some stuff. I love you and can't wait for you to be my wife."

After he hung up the phone he looked up to see Daniel still listening from the doorway. "So that's our story, huh?" Daniel said.

"Hell, yes. There is no reason for your wife or my future one to know anything about last night. Women don't understand how men are,"

"If you say so," Daniel said.
"Are you saying that you would tell Chris?" Kevin asked incredulously.

Daniel seemed to actually think it over. Finally he agreed. "No way, man. She would not understand at all that it started out innocent. I see so many women at work that she would be forever questioning me about it. No, I say keep it tight."

"That's my man. Hey, you ready to head over to the house? Ashley sounded like she was ready to explode."

Ashley

Never in her life had she been so excited about anything. After the wonderful gift Kevin had given her last night she felt calm and in control. She also realized how much he loved her and knew what she needed. She had never told him how anxious she was but he knew that she needed to get away. She and Chris had had the absolute best time.

Now she asked Katie to turn around so she could tie the huge bow on the back of her dress. She looked so beautiful. Even with her arm in a cast, she looked like an angel. Poor dear was having trouble healing and the orthopedist had hesitated to tell Ashley that Katie may need surgery to correct the fracture. Two more weeks in the cast and then back to see him again to reevaluate. Ashley hoped and prayed that it would be healed by then. Ashley was so proud of her. She was taking her role as flower girl very seriously. She must have walked down the aisle at least twenty times today pretending to throw out petals. Chris had put baby's breath in Katie's hair and it made her seem so angelic and sweet.

"Mommy?" Katie looked up into Ashley's eyes and asked.

"Yes, sweetie," she replied.

"Will we ever get to be together again? I mean, just you and me?"

Taken aback, Ashley waited a moment before she replied. She had assumed that Katie was just as excited about this as she was. Now she wondered if maybe she should have paid more attention.

"Of course we will take the time to do girl stuff alone, honey. Most of the time we will be a family and do things together but sometimes it will be just you and me. Why are you asking?"

"I don't know. I just wondered," she said and then turned and walked off to play with Rosie. Ashley didn't have time to ponder this because just then Chris and her family came into the room. Daniel was gorgeous in his new suit and tie—as was Drew. Chris had spiked Drew's hair up in the front and he looked adorable. He pulled at his collar and winced but she could see that he was proud of himself.

Carley looked so grown up in her lilac dress. Ashley noticed that she had her hair exactly like hers. How sweet! It was nice to have a niece who wanted to look like her. Next came Chris. She was beautiful in her maid of honor dress and her makeup perfect.

"Everybody get out and let me help my sister into her wedding dress, please," Chris ordered. As directed, they all filed out to take their places downstairs.

Ashley felt beautiful in her dress. The feel of the satin and the beads was truly amazing. She could smell the sweet fragrance of the flowers from her bouquet. She went over to the window and gazed down at the people assembled there to witness the marriage. She felt very sentimental and was afraid that she might start to cry and ruin her makeup.

"Feeling emotional?" Chris asked from close by her side.

"Just a little. Excited about the future, yet afraid too. Is that normal?" she asked.

"Of course it is, sweet sister. I only wish Mom and Dad were here. They would be so proud of you." At that, Ashley let a tear slip down her cheek.

"Oh, Chris. Thank you for all the years you have helped me. I don't know what I would do without you."

Never one to put on a big show, she answered. "Same here. Now let's go downstairs and get you married. I hear your music starting up."

The ceremony was short and filled with heartfelt words. Ashley and Kevin had decided to write their own vows. When they had finished, there wasn't a dry eye in the house. Some of the women there may have wished they had the good fortune as to marry a guy like Kevin.

At the reception, there was just as much talk about their house as the wedding itself. People gathered around the food and whispered about the woodwork and the stained glass windows as if they were illegal. Ashley couldn't help but laugh. Funny how people could be jealous. As if just a few months ago she wasn't just an ordinary girl living an ordinary life. How could she have known what was in the stars for her?

"What's so funny, my stunning bride?" Kevin asked as he leaned down for a kiss. "Just all of this," she gestured with her arms to include all the surroundings.

"Are you happy?" he asked.

"You have to ask?" she smiled and looked up into his eyes with the future in hers.

Kevin

How long do these stupid things have to go on? Three hours seemed a little excessive to him. And if he had to answer another question about his training in architecture he would scream. Just nosy people, that was all they were. None of them wanted to know about him as a person. They were just prying for information to gossip about. He and Ashley should have eloped like he first thought.

"I think they are all gone now."

He looked up incredulously at Ashley. "No way. Have you checked the closets?"

At this she threw herself down on the sofa and laughed uncontrollably.

"I take it you don't like crowds?"

"Now, did I say that? I just don't like being around a lot of people at the same time," he said. "Or is that the same thing?" They both laughed and took the other into their arms.

"I think you would stay here forever and keep me holed up here with you. You would never leave and never want to. That's what I think." Ashley smiled, but she gazed into Kevin's eyes in wonder.

"I may just take you up on that suggestion. At least for a few days anyway. Are you sure that Katie will be ok for a few days?"

"Of course. She will be so busy at Chris' house, she won't even miss us."

Katie

She missed her mom. She was at someplace called Honey Moon. She didn't know where that was, but she did know that it meant she was going to stay with her aunt for a few days. She was feeling a little surly. Her arm hurt and itched and she was hungry. Aunt Chris had fixed steak for dinner and Katie hated steak. She couldn't tell her that though because Mom said it was rude to be honest. So instead, she had picked at her food and now she was hungry. She reached for Rosie and petted her sore side gently. In all the chaos, nobody had even noticed that Rosie was hurt. Oh well, better not to have to explain anyway. Who would believe her? She couldn't even believe it herself.

Suddenly there was a knock on the door and Drew came in. She really liked him because he always played ball with her and didn't treat her like a baby. Yesterday he had taught her how to play soccer. That was good for her because now she couldn't use her arm. In soccer you just used your feet. Drew said she was pretty good-for a girl.

"Whatcha up to, girl?" he asked.

"Nothing, just petting Rosie," she said sadly.

"Are you bored?" he asked.

"A little I guess" she replied.

"Want to come downstairs and have ice cream with me?" he offered. This helped her feel better.

"Yes, sure. What kind do you have?" At that she jumped up and ran downstairs.

Ashley

Up the stairs slowly, one by one. He guided her with a gentle hand on her elbow.

"Up, up, there you go."

"I really don't think I need to be blindfolded," she complained.

"Well, I do and I am the maker of the rules. So quit complaining and keep walking," he kidded her.

Finally, she was at the doorway of their new bedroom.

"I think I am getting a nosebleed up here," she joked and pretended to be faint. All joking left her mind a moment later when he revealed her master suite. She stood at the doorway in her wedding dress with her mouth hanging open. Never in a million years had she imagined this!

At the far end of the room was a raised platform to hold the antique white canopy bed. White curtains billowed out from where they were tethered onto the top of each post. The wedding ring quilt on the bed was in her favorite colors of turquoise blue and orange. Above the bed was a photo of her that he had taken last week while she was planting tulip bulbs. Sitting in the dirt and wearing denim overalls, she was looking up at the sky and holding a gardening book. The look on her face was one of true love. To the right was a small sitting area with a working fireplace. He had already started a fire and had lit candles all across the room. To the left was a bay window overlooking the garden. The smell of jasmine permeated the air. On the table was a tray of strawberries dipped in chocolate and a bottle of champagne. She was truly overwhelmed.

When she turned to embrace him he was already waiting with his arms out. "Do you like it?" he had to ask. The answer she gave him required no words.

Chris

She absolutely could not believe Ashley had already quit her job. Two weeks into the marriage, and Kevin was already reigning with absolute power. Of course, if she were honest, she would have to say that Ashley seemed happier than she ever had. Chris was tired of answering questions about Ashley's house, her position at the bank, her new car, her flowers, and her way of life. Seriously, she just wanted people to shut up. Today had been a long day.

Tonight was Carley's band performance. Lately she hadn't been practicing like she should and Chris was afraid it was going to show. Chris had always wanted to be in the band when she was in school but there hadn't been the money. She couldn't figure out why Carley wouldn't be practicing. Give a kid an opportunity and they just act lazy and unappreciative. She let out a tired sigh and went upstairs to Daniel's and her room. He was up there getting ready to go to the school. If she hurried, she might have time for a shower.

Daniel was on the phone, as usual, when she came into the room. Quickly he hung up and turned around to face her. Was that guilt on his face?

"What's up honey?" he asked, a little too quickly.

"Who were you talking to?" she couldn't help but ask.

"Just Jim at work. He needs me to work late for him tomorrow. He's got some kind of function at his daughter's school."

"Again? You just finally had a night off tonight for the first time in a week. I am really starting to hate your new job, Daniel." He bent over to tie his shoes and shrugged.

"Well, sorry, but I've got to cover for him, honey. It's my job."

She was shocked at his lack of response to her outburst. He used to never let her be upset. He used to listen to her when she was worried about something and together they would try to come up with a solution. Now he seemed to take her complaining as part of life and go on. Maybe he was tired of her. She was sure that all those girls at the medical offices were more interesting and better looking than her. And younger. What if he was having an affair? Oh God! She didn't think she could take it if he were. They had been together so long that she didn't know who she would be without him.

"Do you still love me, Daniel?" she asked weakly.

"Of course I do. Why would you ask that?"

"Things just seem different lately. I don't know. I guess it's because the kids are growing up. You get a great, exciting, new job. And here I am doing what I've always done. Cutting and styling hair in the same shop every day. Day in and day out. I am not changing the world or making an impact on anybody any more. Kind of sad if you think about it."

"I think you read too many books. You are working in a hair salon you pinched pennies for years to open. You are doing that because that is what you always wanted to do. You don't have to. You want to. The kids still need you just as much as they ever did before and so do I."

This was the most he had talked to her in a while. Lately he just gave her one word answers to her questions but that had seemed like a real life conversation. Maybe he did still love her after all.

Ashley

She was living in a fairy tale. She got up in the morning and made breakfast for her family and then took Katie to school. Then she would drop by Chris' shop for coffee and a little small talk or go to the market for some grocery items. She would leisurely drive home and go inside to clean up the breakfast dishes. Then she would usually go outside to plant some flowers or shrubs. If it was too cold she would curl up on the sofa with a good book. Sometimes she would nap or cook a new recipe for dinner. Kevin was usually around the house somewhere. Either he was working on the new tool shed out back or up in the study reading. Sometimes they took walks through the woods. Other times they took a drive out to the local theater and watched a movie.

Today was Katie's appointment to have her cast removed and Ashley was planning to pick her up early from school. There were supposed to be some severe storms coming and she wanted to get home before they started. She didn't like to drive in a storm, especially with Katie in the car. She felt so good when she entered the school and signed Katie out for the day. Even though she had grown and changed, the school had not. The smell of the school brought on a case of nostalgia. She remembered being a student here. She even recognized the receptionist as the same lady who used to work here when she was a student herself.

Ashley peeked into Katie's classroom and saw Mrs. McKenzie standing at the front of the room pointing to a list of words. Ashley leaned in and waved tentatively when she spotted Katie among the little heads gathered on the primary colored rug. Katie's eyes brightened when she saw her mom standing in the Kindergarten doorway waiting for her. She jumped up and ran into her mom's arms.

"How about we go get that awful cast off of your arm?" she whispered into Katie's hair.

"Do you think my arm is grown back?" Katie asked. Ashley laughed out loud because no matter how many times she explained the broken arm she couldn't get Katie to understand that her arm wasn't actually broken in half. Funny how little children picture things. Ashley personally hoped that the doctor had good news for them today. Please, Lord, let it be healed, she prayed as the two climbed into the car.

A short while later the doctor pronounced Katie as good as new. She was happy because they let her have a sticker and even begrudgingly thanked the doctor. When they left the building the thunder was beginning and the rain had just started. Katie started begging right away to stop for an ice cream cone. Against her better judgment, she found herself pulling into the local hamburger joint for the treat. She figured that Katie deserved one for being so patient and brave during her visit to the doctor. What difference would fifteen minutes make?

As soon as she opened the door to leave the restaurant she knew she had made a mistake. The wind was whipping the street lights almost horizontally on their wires. The rain had become a torrential downpour that immediately soaked them to the skin. When they were finally buckled into the car, she turned around to see Katie.

"Are you okay, pumpkin?" she asked while wiping the rain from her brow.

"Do you think Rosie is in the house, Mom? Do you think Kevin remembered to bring her in?"

"I am quite sure he did, sweetie. But we will check as soon as we get back home."

Slowly she pulled back into the street. It was raining so hard that she wasn't actually sure where the street was. She relied mostly on memory to find the right side of the road to take. Suddenly there was a gust of wind that pushed the car almost off the road. Hail started pounding the roof of the car and Katie cried out in alarm.

She made a snap decision to take a quick left turn and pulled into Chris' driveway. Far better to stay here through the storm and then go on home later than to chance having an accident. Bracing herself for a good drenching, Ashley opened her door. She saw all the lights in the house go off, just as Chris came running out with an umbrella.

Quickly Ashley got Katie out of the car and into the house. Chris had been about to finish up dinner preparation when the power had gone off. Drew and Carley were gathered in the kitchen and everybody was happy to see Ashley and Katie. Chris took their clothes and hung them up and gave them fresh things to wear. Katie wore an old football jersey of Drew's that hung down to her knees. Katie took a spin to show off her fashionable attire, much to the delight of everyone there. When everything quieted down she remembered that she should call home to tell Kevin where she was. He must be worried. She reached into her purse to get her cell phone, but it wasn't there. She turned out the contents on the kitchen counter. No phone. It must have fallen out of her purse when she was running. Darn! Chris picked up the landline and shook her head.

"Are you kidding? "Ashley asked.

"Nope. I am afraid not. Nothing." Chris replied. The wind continued to wail outside the house.

Suddenly there was a huge crash that rattled the entire house. Crying out in alarm, Katie ran to Ashley. Drew and Carley didn't look like they were very far from crying, themselves. Chris gathered everyone into the hallway and they waited out the storm.

An hour later, the family emerged from the hallway like shell-shocked war heroes. This was by far the worst storm Ashley remembered. She was afraid to even look outside to see how much damage had been done. She was sure that at least one tree had fallen. The main thing was that they were alright.

"Ashley! Come here quick!" Chris yelled from the front door. Ashley could tell by the tone of her voice that something was wrong. Expecting damage from the storm, she jumped up from her place on the barstool and ran to the living room. She came to a sliding stop, and any words she might have had left her. Standing on the doorstep was Kevin. His hair was hanging in his eyes and he was drenched. The look on his face made her blood run cold. He had his head tilted down and his red-rimmed eyes peered up at them steadily. He was repeatedly clenching his hands into fists. She didn't understand why he didn't come on into the room or say something. It was eerie, and she barely suppressed a shudder.

"Kevin? What are you doing? Are you okay?" She moved over to where he stood and ran her hands over him like a mother checking her child for broken bones. The first thing that she detected was the smell of alcohol that surrounded him. She had never known Kevin to drink heavily, so this smell didn't fit with her image of him. She was so confused that she didn't anticipate the blow that landed on the side of her head. Suddenly she was flying sideways into the door jamb with such force the she was momentarily dazed. Her peripheral vision turned black and tried to block out her view, but she knew she must not pass out. Katie was right there screaming in fear and tugging on her arm. She must get up and protect her child from this imposter.

"Get your filthy ass out of my house, you monster!" Chris screamed at him with such fury that even the kids shrank away. She lunged into him and tried pushing him away from them. Kevin brushed her to the side as if she were only a child and reached for Katie. He tugged her thrashing little body into his arms and backed out of the doorway, seemingly unmindful of her pitiful, desperate screams. Katie was fighting him and pleading to be let down. Ashley struggled up to her feet and felt warm blood coursing down her face. Her eyes streamed tears, making it hard to see and she struggled against a wave of dizziness and nausea.

"Where are you going? Come back here with her!" she screamed. She ran out in the rain and tackled him from behind.

"Kevin, what is wrong with you! Please, please stop doing this! What is going on?" She was crying so hard it was difficult to talk. He turned around and the look on his face was enough to stop her from coming any closer. Katie had stopped struggling and was reaching for her mother with both arms outstretched.

At that moment, headlights illuminated them both. Kevin was surprised enough to momentarily release his hold on Katie and she took the opportunity to jump out of his arms and ran into her mothers. Daniel stepped out of his car and looked at everyone as if they were all crazy.

"What is going on here? Will someone please tell me why all of you are in the yard in the storm of the century? Ashley, why are you bleeding? Chris! Someone answer me!" He looked from person to person waiting for answers.

Kevin lunged at Ashley and his fist glimpsed off of her forehead. It was enough to knock her down with Katie in her arms. This was all Daniel needed to see. He took three long steps and planted a right jab directly to the side of Kevin's temple. Kevin's knees buckled and he went down to his knees.

"You! What in the hell do you think you are doing?" Daniel took Kevin's wet shirt into his hands and shook him so hard that his head rolled. Then Daniel punched him with all his fury. Kevin was out like a light and fell onto the ground, limp. Chris ran to Ashley's side and pulled her and Katie into her arms, unmindful of the mud and the rain that was still falling. Everybody was crying and hugging and trying to get Ashley back into the house so they could check her out. Daniel pulled Kevin inside the garage and covered him with a blanket.

"Too good for him," Chris said, as she took her hero's hand in hers and led the way inside.

Chris

Chris had never seen anything even remotely like that in her life. She had never envisioned what it would be like to see a person strike another so hard that their head bounced. People say that television desensitizes people to violence. Now she knew that was not true.

As she lay in bed next to Daniel, she shivered. What would have happened if Daniel hadn't shown up when he had?

"It's over now, Chris. Relax baby. They're okay." He turned over and took her in his arms.

"Why? Why did this happen, Daniel? I mean, one second life was normal and all of a sudden there he was and we will never be the same. I keep replaying it in my mind, wondering what I should have done differently. Why didn't I look out before I opened the stupid door? Why didn't I run for help as soon as it started?"

"We can't live our lives trying to go back and fix the past, honey. Besides, this all happened in a matter of seconds. There is no way you could have prevented this," he said.

"Daniel, you should have seen the whole encounter. Our children witnessed something that was brutal. All their lives we have tried to protect them from this sort of violence and yet now they have seen it here in our own family. What must this have done to them?"

Softly she started to cry.

Katie

Yesterday she had learned that sometimes people can actually split in two. There is the Kevin who helped with her flash cards and who made her breakfast in bed. Then there is the Kevin who hit Mommy last night. The mean Kevin looked like someone on a scary movie. His eyes were red and he swayed when he walked. When he breathed it smelled funny. She was very scared of this Kevin. Mommy said that Kevin was going to go away for a few days to see a doctor. Maybe the doctor would make him better like he had made her arm better. She wondered if Kevin would have to wear a cast too. Would he come home with a sticker?

Mom was so sad. She had stayed in bed all day today. Katie bet that her head hurt. She had a big knot on it where the bad Kevin had hit her. Katie and Sandra had made Mommy get well cards today. Sandra said that they should do quiet things so Mommy could rest. Right now she was throwing a ball for Rosie to chase.

When they finally got home this morning, Rosie was outside, soaking wet and shivering. Katie guessed that the bad Kevin didn't worry about little puppies that were locked out in the rain. He didn't worry about how bad it hurt when he hit Mommy, either.

Ashley

Ashley wondered if it was actually possible for a heart to break. Even after a full day of tearful thought, she still couldn't fathom what had happened. She didn't know how to deal with this sort of tragedy. How would this ever be okay? How would she ever trust him again? Would she even try? How was Katie going to get over this? Would she grow up and choose a man who was abusive because she had seen violence in her own childhood? So many questions. No answers. She was so tired. She picked up the phone and dialed Chris' number even though it was technically way too late to call. The phone was picked up on the first ring.

"Chris?" she said.

"Yeah?" Chris said quietly.

"Thank you."

She slowly put the phone back on the receiver. With the bond the two sisters shared, that was enough.

Kevin

He woke up in jail. He knew this not because of primetime TV, but because it wasn't his first time in one. He looked up to the steel bottom of the top bunk and tried to remember what had happened. Why was he in here? At first, he couldn't even remember his own name. His mouth was dry and tasted like a rotten egg. He smacked his chalky lips and winced when he felt the pain in his lip. Puzzled, he reached up and felt of the swelling and dried blood.

When it hit him he sat straight up and hit his head.

"Oh, my God! Guard! Help! Get me out of here!" he screamed. All he heard was laughing and someone singing down the hallway. The janitor mopping the floor outside the cell didn't even flinch. He needed to see Ashley. What had he done? Was she okay? But mainly, had they already fingerprinted him? Maybe he had awakened on time and this was just a holding cell. Panicked, he started to cry. He slid down the cool concrete block wall and started to bang the back of his head against the wall. The physical pain felt better than the mental anguish. He kept on hitting his head until blood trickled down his back. He vaguely remembered a commotion going on around him. He felt hands touching him and lifting him up onto a stretcher. He felt the prick of a hypodermic needle in his arm. Then he was free.

Ashley

Today she was going to get herself together and take charge of her life again. It had been three days since the ordeal and now she felt ready to face it head on. First, she called Sandra and asked her to come watch Katie. When Sandra arrived, she kissed Katie goodbye and drove over to her sister's house. She wasn't prepared for the devastation the storm had left behind. The huge oak tree that had stood next to Chris' house was down. Branches had torn off shingles and had demolished her niece and nephew's tree house. That must have been the crash they had heard. The local power company had restored all the electricity yesterday. A crew of men was trying to upright the grocery store sign that had been knocked over into the parking lot.

She parked and walked up the sidewalk. She mentally braced herself against the memories and cheerfully greeted Chris.

"Hey, girl. I wanted to see you for a second." Chris moved to let her in.

"How are you holding up, Ashley?" she asked. She moved the newspaper off the sofa so that she could sit down. Ashley's eyes went to the paper.

"Is it in there?" she asked.

"I am afraid so. Page three. "*Local man taken into custody after a domestic disturbance Friday night.*" Ashley cringed and lowered her head into her hands. After a minute she regained her composure and smiled at Chris.

"I am going to be okay, you know. You may not believe it now, but I will survive this. Please try to get over this, Sis. I can only imagine how you must be feeling to have seen that. But, I experienced all of this firsthand and I am going to be okay. I am going to the jail to see him. I will take this one step at a time and deal with it."

Chris was almost brought to tears with emotion. She would have never believed her sister to be this strong. She was a living testimony to strength.

Just then Carley came into the room. She looked at Ashley and winced at the bruise on her forehead.

"Are you ok, Aunt Ashley?"

"Yes, I am fine and Katie is just fine too. I wanted to apologize to you. I know it was very traumatic for you to see, but just know that that isn't normal. Kevin has always been wonderful to me and to Katie. I have never seen violence from him before the other night. Obviously something is mentally wrong with him that I didn't know about, Carley. However, there is no excuse for what happened and he will be punished for what he did."

"I know. I am just so sorry. I never dreamed that Kevin would hurt you." Carley came up to her aunt and gently gave her a hug.

"Time to face the music," she said. She turned on her heel and walked briskly to her car.

Twenty minutes later, she entered the jail and was told that Kevin had been transported to the hospital. Ashley was shocked. Nobody had told her that he was injured, too. Maybe the blow to the head had somehow damaged his brain? Why had nobody told her that her husband was sick? She left the jail and headed to the local hospital. The elderly clerk at the front desk couldn't find Kevin's name on the registry.

"Please look again. I was told that he was brought here by the Clarkston police department three days ago. He has to be here."

"Oh, yes. I remember now. But, he isn't here. He is over at the mental hospital. I work there on the weekends and I always remember names." Ashley could tell that a narrative was going to start from the twinkle in the old lady's eye.

Without waiting to hear her story, Ashley turned and ran out of the lobby. Mental hospital? Well, of course. She raced across the street to the correct medical building and went in to inquire.

"Relationship to patient?" the disinterested man behind the desk asked without looking up from his coffee and danish.

"I am his wife," she responded at first in shame and then she realized that she had nothing to be ashamed of and lifted her chin.

"You can come on back," he said. He reached out and pressed a button on his right and she heard a click. This, she supposed, was a lock release button from the shows she had seen on television. She entered the next hallway and was told to take a seat on one of the primary colored chairs lining the wall. After fifteen minutes, her name was called and she was asked to enter another room. This one was at once more comfortable and warm. A man in a white coat was making notes on a clipboard. He sat behind a dark wood desk. He looked up and smiled. He had a warm smile and his face was very friendly. She immediately relaxed a little.

"Hello, Mrs. Landers. I am Dr. Osgood. I am your husband's psychiatrist and I wanted to talk with you a little bit prior to your visit with him today."

"Of course, Sir. What is wrong with Kevin? I only just learned that he was here."

The doctor looked at her quizzically at this revelation. "Did you not have an encounter with him three days ago that led to the police placing him in custody, ma'am?"

"Yes, Sir. But as you can imagine, I have been very upset by it and I only now decided to go to the jail to talk to him. I thought that they had arrested him on Friday night and he was in jail. They just told me that he was here. I don't know what plans they have for him or why he was brought here."

"I see. Well, given the nature of his diagnosis I don't think it is necessary for this man to be arrested unless you insist. Technically, we call it psychological dissociation. Because he couldn't deal with reality, his mind closed off and shut down. He was unaware of what he was doing and has no recollection of hitting you. Of course, the massive amount of alcohol he consumed didn't help him either. He is much better now than he was a couple of days ago. If you had come in then, I couldn't have allowed you to see him. I think a short visit will be allowed today. As for now, please refrain from bringing up traumatic events. Please don't try to get him to remember you, if he doesn't on his own. Just go in and sit down and let him lead the way. At this point in his recovery, it is very important that he remain calm. Of course we are administering medication to help with this, also. Please be prepared, Mrs. Landers. This is temporary. We hope for a full recovery."

Ashley could hardly walk down the long, sterile hallway. When the doctor opened the door to Kevin's room, the antiseptic smell hit her and almost made her faint. Her husband was really in here?

Dr. Osgood stepped to the side so that she could see Kevin. He was sitting upright in a hospital bed. He was wearing a pale blue gown that buttoned up the back. When he saw Ashley he sat up a little straighter. That was the only indication that he had noticed her. Dr. Osgood went to Kevin's side and leaned down.

"Kevin you have a visitor. Can you say hi?" he asked. Kevin stared at Ashley like she wasn't there.

Somehow, this was more eerie than an angry outburst. His eyes were vacant. She thought that if she had to look into those eyes for very long, she would get lost in the darkness she saw reflected there. It truly broke her heart.

"Kevin? Honey, do you hear me, sweetheart?" she asked. She noticed that she had inadvertently regressed to using pet names with him. How fast we forget she thought to herself. He flinched as if she had hit him and then started to silently cry. Tears coursed down his cheeks unchecked. Dr. Osgood held his hand up to signal to her not to come any closer.

"Kevin, you just rest now. Ashley will come back to see you a little later on, okay buddy?"

The doctor took Ashley's arm and guided her out of the room and down the hallway. He led her into his office and offered her a seat. When she declined, he remained standing too. A true gentleman, she thought. Just like I had thought Kevin to be. When she realized that she had used past tense, she shuddered.

"I can only imagine how hard this has been for you, Mrs. Landers. I am so glad to finally be able to talk to you. I have a lot of questions for you that will help me in his treatment. Has he ever had any sort of problem like this before? Even in childhood?" Ashley was angry because she didn't know. She knew next to nothing about her own husband.

"I am sorry, but I really don't know," she said.

"Maybe I can get his medical records. Who was his doctor before he moved here?" Again, Ashley didn't know. The doctor glanced up from his clipboard to peer at her quizzically. "Do you know where he is from, Mrs. Landers? His date of birth?"

"I know he said his family is from Missouri. I'm sorry. That is all I really know." She knew how this sounded. What had she been thinking? She had married a man whom she knew absolutely no history whatsoever.

"Is there anything I can do to help you?"

"Just make him better, please doctor," she begged. Ashley couldn't be sure but she thought that she saw pity in his eyes.

Sandra

She was trying to braid Katie's hair but the child was unusually antsy today.

"Katie Marie! If you don't stay still it will be night time before your hair is fixed," she reprimanded. Finally she got the elastic band around the end of the braid and let the child up. "Go play, child. Run some of that energy out of you!"

Katie jumped up and ran out the back door with Rosie right on her heels. Hard things that one has seen lately, she thought. No child should have to endure that. So sad about Mr. Kevin. Just proved that you didn't really know anybody.

She climbed up the stairs and began putting away the laundry. Shame that things had come to this. She didn't even know that he was prone to drink. She had never seen empty bottles in the garbage. Nothing to point to this. Poor Ashley! First she had endured all that with Brad, and now this. Seems like some women never win. Humph!

"If I were his mama, I would take a stick to him. Walking two miles in a storm and hitting that girl. Needs a spanking. Drinking and carrying on like that. Maybe he never had a daddy to teach him the right way to act. Boys need their daddies," she mumbled to herself. She hummed a gospel hymn she still remembered from childhood while she worked. She would just say extra prayers for this family. She knew that with God's help, they could overcome.

Kevin

Two weeks was a long time. He was sick of this! It was time to get better. Make a miraculous recovery. He laughed out loud. Around here that was par for the course. People everywhere crying and talking to themselves and laughing at nothing. Gave him the creeps. He missed being at home with Ashley and Katie. He wondered if they would be scared of him when he got home. He hoped not. He really just wanted to get back to normal. Honestly, he hadn't meant to get that drunk. He had started out just picking up a bottle of vodka to sip on at night. He knew that was a bad idea but lately he couldn't seem to deal with some memories that kept popping up. He was just going to relax by the fire and read and sip on his drink. When Ashley and Katie had failed to come home, he had started to get worried. The longer the time, the more he drank. Before too long, he had decided that Ashley was cheating on him and that was why she wasn't home.

He really didn't remember much after that thought entered his head. Everything got mixed up and he didn't remember. He didn't remember heading out into the storm or walking all that way in the rain. He only had a vague memory of hitting Ashley and Katie crying. What a screw up he was! After all his hard work to forget the past, here he was. Just goes to show that you couldn't out run your past. It would always be there to haunt him.

From now on he would have to be more careful to keep that part of himself concealed. It was easy to find a doctor who was willing to work with him and his money. Now it would be a long road ahead to regain all of their trust, but for now he had decided it would be worth the work. Ashley was worth the risk. At all costs he had to keep her from trying to find out who he was.

Chris

She was going to bring that psycho home today. Bring him back into their house and trust him to be good. Chris could hardly keep her mouth shut. Daniel had warned her to not alienate Ashley. He said she needed a friend-not someone to judge her. He said she was a smart girl who knew what she was getting into. Damn, she hated it when he was right. The doctor had assured Ashley that Kevin was back to his normal self now. Chris just worried that his "normal self" was exactly the man they all had seen that stormy night. She felt like her gut instinct had been right all along. She had never trusted that stranger from the beginning. Of course, she didn't anticipate him going absolutely ballistic and trying to hurt Ashley. What had he been going to do with Katie, anyway? Was she the only one who had thought about that?

People around here were too forgiving. Nobody even really knew who he was. All they needed to know, evidently, was that he was charming, gorgeous and rich. She was going to find out though. Just as soon as possible she was going to track down that so called family of his. She wasn't going to stop, even when people laughed at her. She would hire a private investigator if she had to. It was not normal to get drunk and then do what he had done; she didn't care what the doctor said.

She was going to buy Ashley a gun tomorrow. Daniel didn't have to know. He thought she should just go on about her merry way and forget what he had done. She wasn't leaving her family at the complete mercy of that monster.

How would she sleep at night knowing that Kevin was capable of horrible things? What if he snapped again and this time no one was there to save them?

Ashley

She stopped for gas on the way to the hospital to get Kevin. She had planned a special dinner for them to celebrate his return. She had gone to see him yesterday and Dr. Osgood had been right. He must just be one of those people who couldn't drink alcohol. He was so sorry for what had happened. He had cried almost the entire time she was there. It seemed that he couldn't forgive himself. He had asked over and over how Katie was ever going to forget it. The truth was that Ashley didn't know. Katie had been quieter than usual yesterday and today since Ashley had told her he was coming back.

"Is he still the bad Kevin?" she had asked. It had nearly broken her heart to see the pain on her face. She had carefully explained that Kevin had been sick but the doctors had given him some special medicine and now he was better.

Ashley sincerely hoped she was right about that. She had done some serious soul searching about what she should do. A part of her wanted to get a divorce and be done with him. That part of her kept seeing his eyes and felt his hand on her face. She could still feel the utter helplessness that she had felt when he had started to walk away with Katie.

Yet there was the other part of her that loved him so much that she would almost forgive anything for him. She knew that he loved her and Katie from the bottom of his heart. She so wanted to forgive and forget. To be honest, she was almost to the point of exhaustion. She had been unable to sleep for the last two weeks. She had found herself pacing the floor and she kept going in to check on Katie. What had he intended to do with her? She couldn't look past that moment. She didn't want her family to know how torn she was. Ashley acted confident and strong when she was with them, but inside was a totally different story. If she told Chris, she would side with her and try to convince her to leave him.

"Oh, Lord, please help me and give me peace about my decision," she prayed.

Almost as an afterthought she pulled into the pawn shop on the edge of town. Maybe she was forgiving, but she certainly was not stupid.

Sandra

While Ashley was gone to get Kevin, Sandra and Katie made cookies to go with their dinner. It was more of a chore than she expected because she was so worried. She couldn't seem to keep her mind on the task at hand and Katie had looked up at her several times with silent questions on her face.

"Sandra, do you think I will be okay?" Katie asked. Sandra almost dropped the egg she had been holding in her hand. Lordy, that child was intuitive.

"Why, child, why would you wonder that? You know that you are taken care of."

"I keep having those dreams about the dragon. He keeps trying to eat me. Last night, when I turned to look back at him, he looked like Kevin," she said. It was all Sandra could do to keep from crying. What should she do? She had never had a problem she couldn't discuss with Ashley before. This was different. This bordered on sticking her nose in other people's business. Where did you draw the line between a child's safety and people's personal business? For just a second she needed to get out of the kitchen.

"Come here, child. Let's go outside for a little walk. Sandra wants to talk to you." They walked hand in hand out to the swing at the edge of the garden and sat down. Katie was chewing her nails and glancing around.

"Has Kevin ever been mean to you before the other night?" she asked.

"No. Well, maybe one time," she said. Sandra felt her heart jump up in her chest.

"Tell me about it," she pleaded.

"One time he put me in time out for talking sassy to Mommy, but I wasn't being mean. I just wanted to keep watching TV. a little longer." Sandra felt faint. For a second there she had been so scared. Slowly she let out her held breath. Maybe things were going to be okay after all. She glanced at her watch and saw that Ashley and Kevin should be arriving soon. She made her decision right then and there. Wouldn't hurt to just show it to Ashley.

"Hurry up, Katie. Sandra has something she needs to do right quick." They went up the stairs into the house and Sandra gave Katie a quick chore to do. Then, with one last look over her shoulder, she climbed the stairs up to Kevin's study. She was about to open the study door when it opened seemingly on its own. Sandra drew a quick breath and had to sidestep to avoid Ritchie.

"What are you doing here?" she asked in alarm. She had no idea that Kevin's friend was in the house.

Ritchie almost looked guilty. Then, he recovered himself and smiled at the old lady. "Oh, sorry, ma'am. I was just looking for something." Before she could inquire further, he ran down the stairs and out the front door.

Kevin

It was so good to be back home. Honestly, he was sick to death of crazy people, drug addicts and alcoholics. The endless noise and the endless bright lights were enough to almost make him crazy himself. But thankfully Ashley seemed inclined to believe the doctor. He had a year of Alcoholics Anonymous to attend. That was a small price to pay. After he woke up in the jail he knew he had to think fast. The last thing he needed was for these small town cops to try to run a background check on him. He did the first thing that had come to his mind. Act crazy. Crazy people always got let off the hook. Well, maybe not totally. He was sure his recovery wouldn't be overnight. He had a lot to endure because of his temper, but that trait had followed him all of his life.

Truthfully, he was just happy to be home with Ashley. She made him feel good inside. Not the same with Katie, though. Since he had gotten home she hadn't spoken to him yet. She kept sneaking glances at him and once when he had reached for the salt and pepper she had actually ducked like he was going to hit her. What a coward. She had none of the backbone her mother had. Katie must have inherited some traits from her sorry father. That was too bad. He had just started to like the kid, too. Oh well. Never one to dwell on negative things, he decided to ask Ashley if she wanted to go for a walk. That should clear his head. He needed to think things through. Somehow, he had to regain Ashley's trust. He knew Chris was going to be a problem. He would just keep his wife away from her from now on. For now, he just wanted to see where they stood. When they were far enough away from the house to be out of ear shot, he stopped walking and turned to take her hand.

"Ashley, I didn't want Sandra to hear this, but I have a reason to suspect that Chris set me up."

"What on earth are you talking about?" she asked in alarm.

"Well, I would never have told you this if things had went according to my plan, but seems like circumstances have changed. There is not an easy way to say this, so I am just going to be out with it. A few weeks ago I was home alone when Chris came by the house. She had some sort of flowers for you, she said. Naturally, I invited her in and we went to sit in the front room. I thought nothing of it until she got up and then came to sit next to me. Before I even knew what had happened she was all but sitting in my lap and kissing me."

He had to stop because Ashley looked like she was going to faint right there in the road.

"Here, darling. Let's sit down." He led the way to an old log. After he was sure she was okay and listening intently, he continued. "When I yelled at her and pushed her away, she got so mad. She started screaming at me that it wasn't fair that her little sister had everything and she had nothing. Honestly, Ashley, I really thought she was going crazy. I have never heard your sister raise her voice, much less scream like that. Her hair was flying around her face and she was flailing her arms. Finally, I practically threw her out the door into the yard. Just as I was about to slam the door she shouted, "Just you wait, Kevin Landers. I will make you pay for this! Before I am finished with you Ashley will not trust you to even take Katie to school by yourself. Nobody abides a man messing with a little girl! Nobody! Just as soon as I can get her by herself I plan to ruin you!"

"Needless to say, I didn't think she would go through with her threats. I was so stunned by what she had done that I almost couldn't face you that night. What if you saw it in my face and thought I instigated the whole thing? How could I convince you that it was the other way around? I figured you would believe your sister over me. I was so scared for several days there. Then, when you didn't come home that night, I started to worry. What if she had made good on her promise and had turned you against me? I tried and tried to reach you on your phone. Daniel had stopped by an hour before with a case of beer and we had been drinking. The more upset I got the more I drank. I am so sorry honey. I got so stinking drunk that I told Daniel about what had happened. He was mad at me! He said that he believed his wife, the cheater. Then, he stormed out of here and raced out of the driveway. I really don't remember that much after that. I think I passed out for a minute because when I woke up I realized that you still were not home. I must have started walking and ended up at Chris' house. When I saw your car in the driveway, I just knew it was over between us. And to think that you would suspect me of hurting Katie? I was so mad at you for believing her and not even giving me a chance to explain. It was more than I could bear. And then I realized that you would take not only yourself but my little Katie. You would never let me see her again. Oh, Ashley I love her so much. I just wanted to take my sweet daughter and get away from all of you." At this he started to cry. He fell to his knees and laid his face in her lap. They held each other close and cried together. After a moment, he gently pushed her back and wiped the tears from her eyes.

"Do you believe me, sweetheart?"

She didn't have to say a word. She nodded and hugged him close.

Ashley

If she thought she was confused before, now she was dumbfounded. Chris had actually came on to Kevin? She almost couldn't believe it. But, actually when she came to think about it, it did make sense. It would explain why Chris had never liked Kevin. Had she been jealous all along? Warily she rubbed her aching head. She didn't want to believe the worst about her sister. However, she had been complaining lately about Daniel and how she was lonely. But lonely enough to actually try to take Ashley's husband? It would also explain Daniel coming up the driveway and punching Kevin in the face without a moment's notice. Had he known? Even though he had been angry when Kevin told him, maybe he had ridden around town for a while thinking and adding up the facts. From deep within she felt an emotion she had never felt towards her sister before. An incredible rage began in the pit of her stomach.

Chris

Chris was working in the house before actually leaving for the shop. Seems like there was never enough time to get the whole house clean at once. By the time she got one room straightened up, another one was destroyed. She picked up a pair of Daniel's socks that were on the kitchen table. Kitchen table? Why did he leave them there in the first place? Lately he was never home. When here, he was he was so absentminded it was like having a third child instead of a husband. They never had gotten around to that vacation, what with all the problems with Ashley and Kevin. Maybe she would ask him again tonight, if he came home before midnight.

Yesterday at the shop one of her customers had hinted that she had better keep her husband interested. She had said that she had heard about how much he was working and how late he had been coming home. She had graced Chris with the story of how her own husband had been having an affair for two years and she hadn't even known it. Then, she had said that it was always the woman's fault when the man strayed. Chris couldn't blame the poor man. She would have had twenty mistresses if she had been him.

She was putting the socks back in his sock drawer when she noticed a cell phone at the bottom of the drawer. Probably an old one that they didn't use any more. Why was it in here? Curious now, she turned the power on the phone and was surprised to see that it was charged up. She didn't recognize the number that came up. A faint feeling of suspicion started in her. A part of her wanted to just put the phone back in the drawer and go on about her day. But, of course she couldn't do that. She pressed the button that listed saved numbers but there were no entries. She hit the redial key and it pulled up a familiar number. It took her a minute to recognize Ashley's cell phone number. That was strange but not suspicious. They all had each other's numbers and called as needed. She tried the text messages. Two messages had been saved. Number One: "Meet me at eight." Number Two: "Had fun. Might be able to break free again tomorrow around lunch time. Will call later."

Both were from Ashley's cell number.

Frantically she scrolled down to see the date they had been sent. Three weeks ago? Why would Daniel be meeting with Ashley?

She needed to sit down. She was sure there was a good explanation for this. Instead she reopened the dresser drawer threw all the socks out onto the floor. A pair in the back seemed too heavy. She put her hand up in the sock and withdrew a piece of paper and a key. The note was handwritten and had been torn off of a note pad of some sort. She recognized it as the note pad on Ashley's refrigerator with birdhouses down the side. Ashley used it for her grocery list. "Just in case I am in bed when you get here, feel free to come on up." With a key.

Chris ran to the bathroom and threw up. The bitter taste of acid burned her mouth. Tears ran from her eyes and down her face. She curled up onto her side and didn't move from that spot all day. She could try as she might to explain this, but there was no denying that Ashley and Daniel were involved. Dear Lord.

Kevin

Well that little detail had been taken care of. He needed Ashley at home and away from her nosy family, and he had obtained that. It had been easier than he had expected and he was glad. He really didn't want to have to get ugly. Just a little infidelity and both the girls were thrown for a loop. So easy. These small town girls couldn't abide any sort of conflict. Manipulation was just simply putting a suggestion in somebody's head and the rest was history. They took that and ran with it. His work was done. Sighing in contentment, he reached over and put his arm around his precious wife. She smiled in her sleep and cuddled up a little closer to him, but even in sleep her brow was creased in worry.

Those first few days had been hard on her but he could see that she was really happier with just him and Katie. She didn't need her sister anyway. All she did was cause problems and keep Ashley confused. Better to just keep her at home where she belonged; where she was needed and cared for.

As for Chris, she had done just as he expected and not said a darn word to Ashley. Things could have turned out a little differently if she had decided to confront her. But he had been banking on the fact that she would be more hurt than angry. Same as Ashley. When her best friend did something so terrible, she had hidden and silently cried. Hurt was a strange thing. It made people quiet and reflective and usually could never be forgiven—even if people promised they would.

Ashley

She was trying her best to get on with her life. And to think that she had almost lost the person who loved her most. How a life could be completely changed in the blink of an eye. She had thought she should be scared of Kevin, yet he was a victim just as she was. She knew some people would argue that he had no excuse to have hit her, but she knew he never would have done it under normal circumstances. Rage could drive a person to do things he normally wouldn't even consider. Several times a day, she would start to call Chris, and then be shocked all over again when she realized that she would never be calling her. She was a traitor of the worst kind. Ashley didn't want to even hear her side of the story.

From upstairs she heard Katie calling to her. She climbed up and entered Katie's room to find that Rosie had chewed up a Barbie doll. All that was left was part of a leg. Katie was scolding Rosie. "Rosie, you chewed up my favorite Barbie doll. I have left toys all over the house that you can play with. Why did you have to do this? I am afraid that you will have to go to time out."

When she looked up and saw her mother she started to cry.

"There, there sweetie. Don't worry and be angry. Dogs have a hard time deciding which things are ok to chew on. If you had remembered to pick up your toys like I asked, this wouldn't have happened. Here, help me clean up the mess."

"Let's go out to dinner and do some Christmas shopping tonight. What do you say? Let's go ask Kevin what he thinks about it?" Hand in hand the pair went back downstairs to find him. He was in front of the fire reading a book about refinishing furniture.

"Want to take a break from that fascinating book and go shopping?" Ashley asked.

"Sure, if that is what my bride wants to do. How about you, Katie? Are you up for some shopping? Better get started on the Christmas list. Won't be long before Santa comes to town."

"Yippee! Let's go, let's go!" She had already started running for her shoes before the adults could bat an eye.

"I take it that is a yes?" Kevin had to ask. Ashley went to him and sat down In his lap.

"Are you sure you feel up to it, honey? I know you have been tired lately."

"Oh, no. Let's get out of this house. I'm starting to feel a little cooped up."

Carley

She had decided that she was never going to get married. Never. All that came out of love was hate. Better to just stay away from men at all. All of her friends at school drooled about this boy and that. They listened to Justin Bieber and watched videos all day long. They fanaticized about kissing and stuff. Ashley felt older than any of them. Of course, she had seen what love could do to a person.

If she were honest, she would say that life sucked. She smiled when she thought of what Mom would say if she knew that Carley used words like that. It seemed like everything had changed lately. Mom and Dad didn't speak to each other, ever. They moved around each other like they were just inanimate pieces of furniture. When they noticed one of the kids watching they would put on a fake smile and talk too happily and loudly. Who did they think they were kidding? She and Drew weren't stupid. It made her mad. Mom should tell them what was going on.

Actually, she had asked Dad about it last week. He had been on the phone when she went into the kitchen for a snack. He hung up quickly and smiled at her.

"Dad, what is going on around here?" He had acted like she had shot him. His eyes darted around the room as if he were looking for a place to escape. Finally, finding no one to rescue him, he had pulled out a chair. He grabbed a bag of cookies from the pantry and gestured for her to sit.

"Sit down, honey, and let's talk. Uh, there are times in every family when things just feel different. This is completely normal. Mom and I have just discovered some differences and we're discussing them openly and trying to decide what the best way to handle them. We aren't mad at each other. We are definitely not angry at you or Drew. This is adult stuff that we just have to work out. I am sure that in a few weeks, everything will be back to normal."

Having said this responsible, rehearsed speech he leaned back in his chair with a satisfied and relieved look on his face.

"So, are you and Aunt Ashley having an affair or not?" she asked brutally. Let him squirm, she thought.

Dad had coughed and choked on nothing for a full minute. Then he looked up at Carley and she thought maybe he was seeing her for the first time in a while. He studied her face so intently that she was embarrassed and had to look away.

"Come here, Carley. Sit on my lap like you used to do when you were little."

With a quick look to be sure Drew wasn't around, she did as asked. It felt good to be held again. She was tired to death of being worried and confused. Maybe now she would have some answers after all.

"Carley, I didn't realize you knew so much. I won't even ask how you know about what your mom and I have been fighting about. Let me just say that this is between your mother and me. There has been a terrible misunderstanding, that's all. I don't even understand how some things have happened around here. I won't go into the details with you now. Just know that I am an honest man. I would never do anything like that to your mother. Please believe me when I say that I love her with all my heart." Carley let out a sigh of relief.

"Well, why don't you tell her that?" she laughed. "That's easy-tell her she was mistaken and then we can get back to normal."

Her father seemed to remember that she was only twelve years old then. He smiled at her and patted her back. "I wish it were that easy," he said. If only the world worked like that.

Sandra

She would have the night off tonight, it seemed. Kevin had called and said they had decided to go out so they wouldn't need her tonight. She hoped it wasn't something she had done. Or that they had found out something she had done. Heavens, she would be nervous as a cat because of that. All these years of living honestly and now she had done something stupid. Stop acting paranoid, you old fool, she mumbled to herself. You're getting worse than an old woman, she laughed.

She decided that since she had the night off she would go do something special for herself. No need to be busy all the time, she thought. I'll just relax and take a hot bath. Make a cake and eat some with a cup of coffee. Heck, I might even paint my toe nails. Her granddaughter always tried to get her to paint her nails. Foolishness! All that vanity. But what's a little fun every now and then? Since Herbert had been gone she had practically thrown herself into helping everyone else. If she stopped for a minute she would have to admit that she was tired.

Katie kept her young and carefree. When she was with her she could just play. They played dolls, cooking, tea party, paper dolls and all sorts of other things. She wished she had had time to play with her own kids like she played with little Katie. Of course, back then she had too much work to do to really enjoy the day-to-day fun of children. Oh, that Katie. Now that child was a sight.

She leaned back in the bathtub and hummed a song to herself. Yes, red velvet cake, she decided. She would eat just a tiny piece and she would take the rest to Ashley and Kevin's tomorrow. She loved that Ashley, but that girl could not cook. Sandra laughed to herself. In my day that would have guaranteed spinsterhood, she laughed. Of course, Ashley was a wonderful mother and wife. To have taken Kevin back after that episode, well that spoke volumes.

Daniel

He was having a difficult time at work, and he didn't really know how to handle the problems confronting him. He had a new job and had told Chris how fulfilling it was, but actually he was starting to hate it. Because he had built it up so much, he didn't know how he would tell her the truth. He wanted her to think he was smart. Truthfully, he felt stupid most of the time. Everyone else in the company except the big bosses were young and confident and had just graduated from college. They were on top of their game, and he struggled to keep up. He hadn't made a commission check last month because he hadn't met the quota.

Now this crazy stuff was happening at home. He honestly had no idea where that phone and note had come from. Someone's sick sense of humor? He was just as shocked as she was. How did a man convince his wife when she had the evidence in her hands? He had tried every night and day, pleading with her, demanding understanding and trust, and arguing with her. Did Chris really think he would stoop so low as to mess around with her sister!? Even slime bags had limits. He loved Ashley, but not like that.

On the heels of that catastrophe with Ashley and Kevin, he had to wonder who had put it there. Something was up, and it wasn't just a game. Unable to come up with any explanation for all of this, Daniel rubbed his eyes and leaned back into the sofa.

His troubled mind slipped back to his worries about work. Nobody at work asked him to cover for them anymore. One screw up with a sample of medication to the wrong doctor and that trust had been broken. Daniel rubbed his eyes and sighed deeply. He wondered if things would ever be good again. Even his own daughter thought he was no good. As far as he knew, Drew didn't know anything about all the turmoil. Thank goodness for that.

Time to take Drew to school for the art show. Kids making refrigerator art, and the school selling parents their own kids' work for big bucks-that was enterprising! What parent could pass it up? Obviously not his family. He looked up above the sofa at Carley's artwork from last year. For the first time he really looked at it. Man, that was good. Really good, talented. Funny how he had never noticed his daughter's ability before. He wondered why she never mentioned how much talent she had. He thought he might ask her about pursuing art. Goodness knows he understood about wanting to make sure you went after what really meant something to you. He had given up drafting in high school because his parents could have never afforded architecture school. He would be sure that his children really put a lot of thought into their future and did what called them. He wanted them to live life to the fullest and never settle.

Misty Erwin

Chris

Chris had decided to clean out the refrigerator. Dirty job, but somebody had to do it. The house pretty much sparkled. She had to keep busy or risk having to think. For instance, today she was cleaning out her dresser drawers and decided to take a break. As soon as she sat down and closed her eyes she wondered if Ashley had ever found her cell phone. She had said that it had fallen out of her purse that night of the storm. Like lightening had struck her, she had jumped up and started to work again. She had sworn not to think about Ashley any more, ever again. Too painful.

She realized that her hands were shaking again. More and more lately she had trembled. Just tired and hungry she thought. Better get a sandwich. That might help. When was the last time she had eaten anyway? She struggled to remember if she had had dinner last night. If Ashley hadn't even had her cell phone when those messages had been sent, then something was badly wrong-darn it! Why couldn't she leave it alone? She always tried to rationalize people's actions and forgive them. She put the mayonnaise on the bread and started layering the ham. But, if she didn't ask her about it, how could she honestly live with herself? Especially since she had remembered later that Ashley couldn't even find her phone that night when Kevin had came.

Chris gave up and sat down at the table to think. Time for reckoning. It was high time to go see Ashley and just get all of this out in the open. Even if they fought and never spoke again, it would be better than this. They had always been too close to let it end without a battle. This decided, she smiled for the first time in weeks. She got up and got her coat from the hall closet and went outside. The sandwich was left uneaten on the kitchen counter.

Daniel

He was worried. Chris had confided tonight that she had intended to confront Ashley today. She had made it as far as the end of the driveway before she had succumbed to fear. Now she said that she was going to go over to her house tomorrow, hell or high water. She looked resolute and calm. She was going to do it.

Not that he had anything to hide. But, something really bugged him about the whole situation. He had racked his brain all week trying to figure out just what in the heck was going on around here. First, a mysterious cell phone and note with damning evidence was in his sock drawer. Someone had obviously put it there. Why? Why would anyone want to break him and his wife up? He just couldn't come up with a valid reason. They had been together since high school and had not ever had so much as had a big fight.

Next, why hadn't Ashley called or came over to the house? She didn't know about all of this. He had tried and tried to convince Chris that this was a stupid joke but she was having none of it. He knew for a fact that the only relationship he had ever had with his sister-in-law was strictly one of friendship. That meant that Ashley had nothing to hide and he knew it. Why all of the sudden had she stopped all contact with Chris? It looked damning. The fact that she stayed away looked suspiciously like she was caught and scared.

It was starting to look like he had been asking the wrong question. Not why, but who? Who would want to break them up? Suddenly he stood to his feet in shock. When all the dots were connected it made more sense. Not who wanted to break up him and Chris, but who would like to see Chris and Ashley at odds?

When put that way he was worried. There was only one person who had a problem with the sisters and he wasn't the most reliable person around. Suddenly he was scared. Not scared like when you have a nightmare as a child, but when you are suddenly cast right into a nightmare as an adult.

Ashley

She was washing Katie's hair in the tub when the doorbell rang. Late at night for a visitor, she thought. She stood up and grabbed a towel for her hands and started down the hallway towards the stairs. Right as she was about to turn the corner and go downstairs, she heard Kevin talking. Oh, so he was inside. She thought he was out in the garage. Who was he talking to?

She leaned out to see who their visitor was and was surprised to see Daniel at the doorway. He had dark circles under his eyes, was wringing his hands and he had lost weight. What had happened? She wondered. She felt bad for not talking to him anymore. She had always had a good relationship with him. It wasn't his fault that his wife was a cheating traitor. With words of greeting on her lips she started down the stairs. Suddenly she stopped before she was seen. Kevin was leaned in close to Daniel and was talking in a low voice and she had to struggle to make out his words.

"Yeah, she has been so sick lately," Kevin said. "I honestly have been so worried. After all that happened before, I thought things would get back to normal. But she just gets worse and worse. I'm thinking of having her committed," he said quietly.

Who was he talking about?

Daniel looked stunned. "I'm sorry. I didn't know about it. I am sure that Chris didn't either or she would have understood what was going on. Did you know that someone hid a cell phone in my sock drawer? It had messages from Ashley to me. Chris has been so devastated. She thought we were having an affair."

At this he put his face in his hands. Kevin moved to thump him on the back.

"Please tell Chris that what Ashley needs right now is just some time alone. She is going to therapy seven days a week. I don't know what caused this relapse. The doctors said that they had been treating her for several years with drugs, but obviously they are no longer working. I have caught her doing the strangest things. I honestly have begun to worry about leaving her alone with Katie."

Daniel couldn't seem to follow the conversation. "Like what?"

"Well, one day Katie was playing with Rosie and out of the blue Ashley just stuck out her foot and tripped her. Acted like it was an accident but it obviously was intentional. I saw her do it. Made me wonder about that broken arm. I came home several weeks ago and found her in bed with my best friend, Ritchie. I have never been so upset in all my life. That was the day I came to your house. I am so sorry for that terrible night. I should have controlled myself better but just the vision of him and her together was enough to almost drive me to a nervous breakdown. I mean, for goodness sakes, he was my best friend!"

"Oh, man. I am so sorry about all of this. I had no idea. I am baffled. Sorry I came over here. I just wanted to warn Ashley that Chris is coming over. I will go home right now and tell her about what is going on. Have the doctors said how long her treatment may take?"

"Hard to say. Depends on how soon they can find the trigger and how she can come to terms with her past." He put his face in his hands and rubbed hard as if to clear a bad memory.

"I guess Chris has told you about their dad molesting them? I know how close you are and I am sure that Chris has talked with you about it over all these years, but I really had no idea. I was blown away. Poor girls."

"What? Oh, God. Please don't tell me anymore. I need to get home and think. Please give Ashley my best. If you need anything from us, please don't hesitate to call."

With that, Daniel practically ran out the door into the night.

Kevin

That should keep the clan away for a while. He should have written movie scripts, he thought with a chuckle. If this lifestyle falls through, he might move out to Hollywood and give it a try. He could give Steven Spielberg a run for his money. Mental collapse, child abuse and molestation would make a great movie, he thought. When he heard Katie call to Ashley he looked up. Maybe he would go help Ashley get the child ready for bed then he would make them all popcorn and they could watch a movie together.

Just the three of them.

Chris

Daniel was acting strange tonight. He had gone out supposedly for a gallon of milk an hour ago and came back in pale as a ghost. She wondered if he had another fling going. Wouldn't surprise her. Anybody who would mess around with his wife's sister would not hesitate to go for it again with someone else. She could hardly look at him anymore. To tell the truth, she was repulsed by him.

"Chris, I need to talk to you, honey," he said, "after the kids are in bed."

A while later, he took her hand in his and tugged her towards their room.

"I don't know what you are up to, Daniel, but don't even think about going into my room," she said with anger. Since the blow up, Daniel had been banished to the couch.

"Ok. Ok. Stop being so hateful. Let's sit on the sofa, then." Quietly she went to do as he asked.

"If you are going to tell me you are having an affair, you can spare me. I already know about it."

"Chris, SHUT UP! Just shut your damn smart mouth for one minute and let me talk for a change. I am sick of this shit. I am sick of being made to feel dirty. I am sick of the sly looks you are passing my way. I am sick of my own children accusing me of screwing your sister. This shit is over! I mean it. For good. If you think you can bully me into admitting to an affair I haven't been having, you are wrong. Maybe I have cowered to you and bent to your demeaning remarks before, but now I am sick of it. If you don't be quiet for a minute and let me talk, I am moving out tonight."

This said, he collapsed on the couch as if someone had let the air out of him.

Chris had seen his defensive stance with his hands clenched into fists and the horrible scowl on his face, and she was dumbfounded. As much as she had daydreamed about him moving out and their impending divorce, she had not had the nerve to actually picture this. He was serious, too. She had known him long enough to know when he meant business. She was scared. She had never been as scared in her entire life as she was this minute. Daniel was her rock. He was all she wasn't. He was strong and dependable, calm and patient. He didn't deserve to be treated like she had treated him, especially when she realized that she now believed him. The tears started and couldn't be stopped. Before she could change her mind, she bent over and put her arms around his waist. It felt so good to touch him again. He looked over in surprise.

"I am so sorry, Daniel. I have treated you like a horrible person. The truth is that I don't really even believe all this myself. I don't know how that phone got in your drawer, but I don't believe you and Ashley were having an affair."

Daniel couldn't believe his ears. She believed him? He hadn't expected her to succumb so easily.

"What? You believe me?"

"After that outburst, how could I not?" she smiled. "Thank you so much for not leaving me. I know that I have been terrible to you. I am ashamed for not believing in you. I was just so scared that it might be true. The evidence was in my hand, which was hard to deny. But one thing I can't deny is the power of our love. When I touch you, I feel your heart." She stood up and took his face into her hands. She peered deeply into his open, honest face. Then she clasped his hand in hers. "Let's go back to my room after all," she said.

It was late. Chris could see the moon up in the sky through their window. Looking at the moon had always made her think about mortality. Made her feel so small and insignificant. Like one of a trillion people in the world. A nobody. Just a brief thought in the scheme of the whole world.

"Why are you sighing like that? Pleasure or worry?" Kevin asked as he brushed her hair back from her eyes.

"Both, it guess. Daniel, I didn't know Ashley was having problems. I didn't see it. I am her sister and her best friend and I didn't see it. Instead I almost alienated my husband and I have practically abandoned my children. What kind of person am I?" softly she cried.

"You are a wonderful wife and mother who had to face something she never thought she would face from two of the most important people in her life. You had no way of knowing, Chris. People with mental problems figure out ways to hide them from the world. She was struggling. I, for one, am happy that Kevin came along and is helping her. No telling what may have happened."

"Will she be okay? Did Kevin seem like he was worried or just angry? Here he just marries Ashley and this happens. Did he say what caused it?" she asked.

In the dark, Daniel looked away from the silhouette of his wife's face. "No, he didn't," he said.

Katie

It seemed like forever since she had left the house. She and Kevin and Mom never went anywhere any more. Sandra had almost stopped coming over, too. She had shown up yesterday with cookies, but Kevin had met her at the door and taken then cookies. They had talked in low voices that she couldn't understand and then Sandra had left.

Mom had stopped shopping and planning Christmas. She wondered if Santa would still come if they didn't have a Christmas tree. Kevin had told her that Christmas was three days away, but she couldn't get excited. Usually she and Mom had special things to do. They always planned a special dinner with Aunt Chris and Uncle Kevin and her cousins. Sometimes they even invited their neighbors to come. All the kids played and ran around the house. After the adults finally got finished eating, they gathered the kids around the tree and gave out gifts. Last year Katie had gotten a handmade doll. She still played with it all the time. Rosie had actually chewed on the dolls right arm a little bit, but that was okay. She loved her anyway.

Katie was worried about Mommy. She stayed in the bed all the time now. Kevin said to be extra quiet because Mom needed to rest. Whenever Sandra called, Kevin told her that he and Ashley were fine without her today. Katie had heard him tell her that after Christmas she would be needed to watch her again. After Christmas. That was a long time away. She missed Sandra. Surely Sandra missed her too. They had been in the middle of reading a good book too.

Katie wondered if Mommy was okay.

Against Kevin's orders, she crept up the stairs into Mommy's bedroom.

"Mommy?" she whispered. Nothing. "MOMMY!" a little louder this time. The quilt on Mommy's bed moved a little. This was all the invitation she needed. She ran up the step to the bed and jumped up on the mattress. "Are you okay, Mom?" she asked timidly. Her mommy looked up through squinty eyes and for a minute Katie didn't think she knew who she was.

"Katie, are you okay, sweetie? Please talk to me before Kevin comes in here. Where have you been?" Her mom seemed scared. Maybe she hadn't meant to sleep so long. Sometimes Katie felt funny when she overslept, too.

"Mommy, get up. You've been in here too long. Why are you sleeping so much?" Before she could answer Rosie began barking at the door. Seconds later Kevin appeared at the doorway as well.

"What are you doing up here, Katie Marie. I thought I told you to stay away from your mother. She needs to rest."

"No, no, Kevin. Please let her stay. She isn't bothering me. Please?" Ashley pleaded. Katie looked from Kevin to Mom in surprise. Never before had she seen her mother act like Kevin was the boss over her. She almost acted like she had that night at Chris'. This scared Katie a lot so she snuggled up to her mother.

Ashley

Ashley had never dreamed of getting a five year old involved in such as this. Katie deserved a normal life and it was her fault that her daughter had to deal with this. She must think!

"Katie, will you please go get Mommy a wash cloth with cold water on it, please?" Katie jumped up, pleased to have something useful to do. Ashley slapped herself on the cheek and rubbed her eyes.

"Dear Lord, please help me get out of this mess. I don't know what he has done to me," she prayed.

She could never remember feeling quite like this before and she wondered what day it was. Actually she was almost scared to ask. She could tell by the flatness of her stomach that she hadn't eaten in a while.

When Katie came back to the bed with the cloth, she pressed it upon her brow and waited for her head to clear. Out of the corner of her eye she saw Katie watching her.

"Katie, what have you been up to? Did Sandra come today?" She tried to act normal but it was so hard with her head so groggy.

"Mommy! Sandra hasn't been here in ages. I've just played with Rosie and watched TV. Kevin fixed me a sandwich to eat. I'm bored. Let's go Christmas shopping. And we need to get a Christmas tree. We only have three days to get it all done."

Ashley felt herself blanch. Three days? That couldn't be possible.

That would mean that days had passed. She could only remember bits and pieces of things lately. She remembered Kevin lifting her head and spooning something into her mouth. She barely remembered stumbling to the bathroom. What in the world had happened to her? Had she had a stroke? Then, she remembered the last thing she had seen. What was Daniel doing there? Slowly she connected the dots. When the realization hit her, she began to cry.

Sandra

It wasn't normal. No, not normal at all. Something wasn't right with this picture. She had always helped Ashley with her Christmas shopping, cooking and planning. Always. She didn't think getting married would change someone so much. Why, everyone knew how much Sandra loved Ashley and Katie. She practically worked for free because she needed them as much as they needed her. Yet every time she called over to the house Kevin answered and practically hung up on her. She was having no more of his shenanigans. That man needed to be put in his place. She should have done it weeks ago when he hit Ashley. No sir, that wouldn't do at all.

She decided to make cupcakes. Red velvet was Katie's favorite. She would make cupcakes, take them to Katie, and check on Ashley and Katie. If that Kevin answered the door again and hedged about letting her in, he would just get a piece of her mind. Maybe if she were lucky Ashley would ask her to help out with something. She was bored at home. When she had mentioned all of this to her children on Sunday, they had told her to leave the newlywed couple alone. To be honest, she didn't want to. She wanted to be a part of their family like she had always been. She wondered if Katie was still having nightmares. Goodness she worried about that child. Such a sweet girl. Yes, she certainly would just go on over there and see about them.

Carley

Carley walked through the stores without really seeing anything. To tell the truth she didn't care about Christmas this year. Nothing was the same around the house anymore. She'd rather be at her friend's house than at home any day. Most of her friends only lived with one of their parents or some lived with their grandparents. Secretly she envied them. At least they didn't have to pretend that everything was fine and the world was a happy place. She envied them also because if they had a fight with their mother they could just go to their dad's house to stay. When her friend Stacy fought with her mother, her dad always took her shopping or skiing or something fun. He always seemed glad to see her and welcomed Carley to come with them any time she wanted to.

Carefully she touched a ceramic ornament that hung on an artificial Christmas tree. She heard a child talking in the next aisle over. "Let's get mommy a new robe, Kevin. She needs a new one because she stays in bed all the time. Let's go get her a nice new pink one. One that is soft and pretty. She will love it so much. I just know she will. We could also get her new . . . ." the little voice stopped mid-sentence when Carley stepped around the end of the aisle.

"Carley! I miss you!" Katie yelled and ran up to Carley to hug her. Carley stooped down to meet Katie.

"Katie, hey cousin. What have you been up to?"

"Nothing. I haven't left home since, I don't know, weeks or months or something. Mom is sick and can't get out of bed. She cries all the time and Kevin acts mad."

Katie stopped when Kevin stepped up to her and put a protective hand on her shoulder. Carley could see that he was hurting her and sure enough Katie winced at the pain.

"What are you doing?" she asked boldly. Seeing him grabbing her little cousin caused her to sound angry.

"Taking my daughter shopping. Now let's get going, Katie. We still have a few more shops to look at."

Roughly taking her hand in his, he turned and started walking away.

"Kevin?" she called. When he turned, she did something she had never in all her life dared to do. She lifted her hand and extended her middle finger. Surprise registered on Kevin's face before it turned to anger and then finally admiration. He smiled at her in a way that stopped her heart.

When Katie and Kevin were gone, Carley darted into a restroom and hid. For some reason she was scared. Mom had said that Aunt Ashley was sick, but she wondered. Why would she all of a sudden get some kind of mental disorder? Carley had never known her to be even a little nervous or worried. She was a wonderful mother and Carley couldn't believe it when she had heard her mom and Dad whispering that maybe Ashley had somehow had something to do with Katie's broken arm. That was just plain ignorant if they asked her.

Of course, nobody asked her. She was invisible. Slowly, she regained her wits and left the restroom. Before meeting her mom in the designated spot, she had one more place to go. She was going to go buy Katie a Christmas present. Her mom had said that this year they would leave the new family to themselves, but Carley had made up her mind. She was going to go see her aunt and cousin. She was going to go see just what Katie had been talking about. She went into the toy store and looked for Katie a new Barbie doll. This one was a flower girl. She knew how much Katie had loved being the flower girl in her mom's wedding. Thinking about all the problems her family had had since that day, she put the doll back on the shelf. Maybe a nice pad of paper and some new crayons would be better. Yeah, she thought, maybe Katie might want to forget about that wedding.

Chris

Chris was excited about tomorrow. Ever since she was a child, she had loved Christmas. She had been seven when her parents had been killed, but she clearly remembered them. She had always been disappointed that Ashley's memories were so vague. Of course, at four years old, not much made an impression. Chris remembered when her mother had decided to take the girls out into the woods to cut their own tree. Chris didn't remember what circumstance required them to do this chore alone, but she did remember that her Dad wasn't there. Mom had let her carry the saw and Ashley had carried twine to bind the limbs up with. The air was crisp and cold and the birds were singing. It seemed like it had taken hours to find the perfect tree, but surely it was only minutes. Time could be construed in a child's mind like that. They had cut and cut on the trunk of the tree but couldn't get it to saw off. She remembered her mother sitting down in the leaves and starting to cry, but Chris didn't know why. She thought that it was silly to cry over a tree.

Now, looking back with an adult's knowledge, she wondered what had been wrong. Why had her mom not waited on Dad to come with them? What had caused her to cry? She tried to imagine what her mother had been like but she was sad because her memory was dim.

Oh well, no need for being sad. Today was Christmas Eve and it was a busy day. She had closed her shop today and tomorrow so she didn't have to worry about that. She needed to go finish up her grocery shopping. Carley bounced into the kitchen and asked, "Mom, I need a favor."

"Ok, what's up?"

"I need you to take me over to Aunt Ashley's house. I bought Katie a present and I want to give it to her." Chris studied her daughters determined face and wondered where the girl got her nerve. She had always been so brave and tenacious. Whatever she had put her mind to, she had gotten.

"Carley, I really don't think that is a good idea. Kevin said that Ashley was having a hard time right now. I don't want to make her any worse and to be honest; I am a little scared for you or me to see her like this." This revelation made Chris have to suddenly fight back tears. Her throat hurt from the pain of trying to avoid crying. Why did it always have to be that someone made her sad just when she had regained control of herself?

"Mom, I really want to go over there," Carley said belligerently.

"And I said no. Carley, look at me and stop rolling your eyes. I said no, and I mean it. Do not go to Ashley's house. I will decide when the time is right for us to visit."

With that she went back to her grocery list.

Kevin

Things seemed to be a little more worrisome than he would like. Ashley had been sitting up in bed some today. When he came into the room, she always seemed a little scared at first. May be time to up the medication, he thought. Only good thing that came out of that little stunt in the mental hospital was the drugs. They really should keep a more watchful eye out. It would be easy for some mental case to snatch some powerful medication and nobody would be any the wiser. He laughed to himself.

He found himself a little nervous. Katie was being a nuisance. She wouldn't stop nagging him to come up and see her mom. That stupid dog of hers was chewing up everything in the house. Sandra kept calling and calling. She wanted to come over too. Now Carley had been at the store and pretty much slapped him in the face. Why wouldn't people leave them alone? What was it about his wife and daughter that made people so possessive of them? Seems like anybody who ever ran into them was calling or knocking on the door. Some jerk she used to work with had even come calling with a fruit basket. That one had almost sent him over the edge. Maybe it was high time to move on. Just pack up and hit the road. There was certainly nothing here to hold them. Nothing but pain and misery. All they wanted was a little peace and quiet.

Ashley

Social services had been out yesterday. Seems that someone had reported her for child abuse. They had asked her question after question about Katie and her broken arm. She had tried really hard to answer their questions the best she could, but some of the words just wouldn't come out right. She knew that she was slurring her speech and sounding lame, but she just couldn't get a grip on herself. She knew that she must look a mess. Her hair was dirty and tangled up. Her clothes were wrinkled. What would they think of her? It seemed like they had stayed for hours and hours and by the time they left, she was so sleepy. She didn't really remember what had happened right after they left. She vaguely remembered Kevin talking to one of the ladies in a low voice. She thought she heard words like drugs, mental problem, and bad episode. Who was he talking about?

When she had looked over at Katie it was like seeing her for the first time in a while. Was she really that dirty? Her socks didn't match and she had something brown all over her face and hands. Red Kool Aid had dripped on her shirt, too. Basically, she had looked like some kid who nobody took care of. Ashley laughed. Well, that was probably close to the truth. Kevin was too busy doping her up to take proper care of Katie. She laughed again. She heard herself laugh and for some reason she sounded like a crazy person. She rubbed her eyes so hard she saw white spots.

"Ashley, get a hold of yourself," she whispered. Her head hurt so badly that she thought she might start to cry. Get up and move around, girl, she pleaded with herself. You've got to get up and see about Katie. She probably needed help with bathing and dressing and—Christmas! Oh, my goodness! What day was it? Please, dear God, tell her she hadn't missed Christmas.

She crept to the bathroom and turned on the light. Blinded by the brightness, she immediately turned it off again. She peered up at herself in the mirror and gasped. She looked terrible. She looked like a haggard old woman. She splashed cold water on her face and turned on the shower. When she finally emerged from the shower, she felt a little more like herself. Where was Kevin? He usually ran into the room just as soon as she moved a muscle. He had been so attentive to her since this had happened. What exactly had happened?

Too much thinking was causing her to be dizzy so she sat down on her sofa. What were these papers doing here? Looked like legal mumbo jumbo. Carefully she watched her own hand reach out to grasp the papers. She tried to focus on the words but couldn't seem to get her eyes to work.

"Mom?" she heard from behind her.

"Katie? Come on in here sweetheart." She took Katie in her arms and held her. "Katie are you ok?" she asked fearfully.

"Mommy, he is mean now. The bad Kevin came and he lives here now."

Ashley felt her insides turn cold. Before she could fully understand Katie's words the door opened and Kevin walked in.

"Oh, you're up, Ashley. Well, that's good. Do you need anything to eat or drink?" Ashley was so confused. She looked up at Kevin and tried to study his features to see what Katie had meant. She saw only kindness and concern.
"No, honey. Just felt a little better so I took a shower. I can't see well, though. Can you please tell me what happened to me?" she asked.

Gently her helped her up and off the sofa and led her back to the bed. "Don't you worry yourself honey. I have been taking care of you and I think you may be getting better. You just take your medication and lie down for a little while. Don't want you to overdo it."

Ashley let herself be guided and covered up with the quilt. The pillow did feel so good. She could almost drift off again. She felt Kevin's hands placing a pill in her mouth and then the rim of a glass as he held the water up to her dry lips.

Katie

She hated it here. Kevin always smelled funny and he always wanted her to sit on his lap. His breath smelled so bad that she didn't really want to. He loved her. She knew this because he told her so many times a day that she couldn't forget. Sometimes he kicked Rosie. Sometimes he threw the phone and screamed at it. Last night he had gone out for a while and when he came back he was really walking funny. Katie had fallen asleep on the couch watching Dora the Explorer. She had found a pack of Skittles on the kitchen counter and she had eaten those for dinner.

When he came in last night she had hidden behind the couch and waited to see how he was before she came out. He had gone into the bathroom for a minute and then he got a pill out of a bottle and went up the stairs. He heard him walking up the stairs one by one very slowly. Probably going to go give Mom her medicine. Medicine was supposed to make people feel better but Mom wasn't getting better. Katie actually thought Mommy was worse. For a minute she had been better, but then Kevin had came and given her the pill and she had went back to sleep again.

Slowly, Katie had crept out from behind the couch. Rosie had trembled beside her. Poor Rosie. She trembled all the time now. She was scared of Kevin. He walked around mumbling to himself. She couldn't hear what he said, though. Where was everybody? Why didn't Aunt Chris ever come over anymore? What about Sandra, too? Had everybody forgotten about Katie?

Katie had watched a movie one time about a girl who was a hero. She was just little but she was smart and strong. Katie decided that she would do what she could to help her mom. She would be a hero, too. She climbed up on the cabinet and got the medicine bottle. Before she could think about the consequences, she took the bottle up to her room and shoved it as far back as she could under her mattress.

Carley

Christmas had passed without much to mark the passing of the holiday. Everything seemed less and less normal around here. At least Mom and Dad had made amends and were talking again. Drew had been nicer lately. She didn't know what was up with that. Small wonders, she thought.

She really missed Aunt Ashley and Katie. Over the years she had just taken for granted that they would always be a part of her life. She had loved it when Ashley would come over unexpectedly with something unhealthy for dinner. Ashley didn't care what Mom thought. Sometimes she would bring popcorn and lemonade and say that tonight they were going to eat outside on a blanket. Mom always rolled her eyes when Ashley did something like that, but Carley could tell that she loved it as much as they all did. If an offer came up to do anything unusual, Ashley would be the first one to join in. She loved a challenge. Seemed like Katie had taken after her in that respect.

Carley didn't remember that much about Brad except that he was always nice to her. He would pick her up and spin her around in the air when they came over. She remembered that he had left unexpectedly and Ashley had been very upset for a long time. She couldn't really remember what he had looked like but maybe he had auburn hair like Katie did.

It was unusually warm for January. School had already started back after the Christmas break and she was tired. Mom had insisted on Carley trying out for the basketball team and she hadn't the faintest interest in sports. Carley sometimes wondered if she was a big disappointment to her mom and dad. She didn't like band or sports. Those were the things her parents thought kids should be involved in.

Carley decided that since it was Saturday she would take her drawing pad and go for a walk. As an afterthought, she grabbed Katie's unopened Christmas present and stuffed it under her coat. It was a long walk to Ashley's house. She was careful to not be seen. In a town this size, everybody knew everybody else and they would be sure to tell Mom if she was seen walking two miles from home. She saw the house in the distance and stopped to think. What if it were true what Mom and Dad were saying about Ashley? She was a little nervous to be going over to visit. She didn't have any experience with things like this and she didn't really know what to expect.

Slowly she walked up to the house and waited for some sound. After a few minutes it was evident that nobody was home. On a Saturday morning people were usually cooking and cleaning and at least talking to each other. She went up to the window and cupped her hands around her eyes so she could see inside the house. This room was the front living room and it looked like a tornado had come through it. There were clothes all over the place and leftover food containers were strewn on the floor. From where she stood she couldn't see into any other room.

A faint sound caused her to turn around. The little girl standing on the porch resembled Katie, but Carley knew that Katie would never look so bedraggled. Curiously she crouched down to eye level and smiled. Then she realized that this was Katie. She was so skinny and pale. Her eyes were haunted and sad. There was a big bruise on the right side of her face and her right arm hung funny.

"Carley?" she asked. Katie's eyes widened when she realized that it wasn't a dream.

"Katie? What is wrong? What happened to you?" She gathered her cousin into her arms and held her close. Katie looked over her shoulder and appeared ready to jump down and run at the drop of a hat.
"You can't be here. He will see you. He isn't the nice one, Carley. He will hurt you too," she whispered while pulling Carley around the side of the house.

Carley's heart was thumping so hard she could hardly hear her words. "Where is your mother?" she asked.

"Shhhh. Keep your voice down. I think he is asleep. If he wakes up I will be in trouble. Mom is up in the bed. She never gets up anymore."

Suddenly Katie tensed up and froze. Carley looked over her left shoulder and saw Kevin standing behind her. "Carley, honey. What are you doing here?" he asked.

"I just came to see you all for a little while. I brought Katie a Christmas present," she said. She reached under her coat and produced the brightly wrapped package.

"Well, that is nice of you but Katie doesn't need any more toys. She leaves them laying around the house and that dog of hers chews everything up. I hate to cut the visit short, but Katie and I have some business to attend to. You be running along now. Tell your mom and dad we said hi."

Carley turned and began to back away. Kevin's eyes were bloodshot and red. He couldn't stand up straight and was staggering around. She didn't like the way he kept staring at her. She was scared.

"Ok, Uncle Kevin. Good to see you both. Tell Ashley I hope she feels better soon. See you later." She hugged Katie close and whispered in her ear. "I will go get help." She nodded at Katie to assure her she was telling the truth but Katie was already shaking her head.

"It will just be worse," she whispered.

Carley waved at them and walked back towards home. What was she going to do? This was serious. Katie was not the same and she had yet to see Ashley at all. Decision made, she ran as hard as she could until she could not breathe and her side hurt. She had slowed down and was trying to catch her breath when a car came along the road and slowed down to a crawl. She didn't care who saw her at this point. She just wanted someone to go help them. Carley looked up to see Sandra rolling down her window.

"Carley, what are you doing out here? I was just going to go check on Ashley and Katie. I intend to see for myself if they are alright. It's been weeks since I've laid my eyes on those two. Want to ride with me?"

Carley could see the intention on Sandra's face. Here was her out. She could go on home and not say anything. To tell anyone she had been there would mean she would probably be in trouble. Sandra was sure to see exactly what she had just witnessed when she got to Ashley's house in just a minute. She was sure that Sandra would follow through with whatever needed to be done. Carley honestly didn't know what should happen next. Sandra would know exactly what to do when she saw poor Katie like that.

In relief, Carley smiled and said, "No, Sandra I was just taking a walk and I am going to the lake to do some sketching." She held up her sketch pad as proof. "You go ahead and let me know how they are, ok? Will you come by our house later on and tell us?" she asked.

Sandra smiled her kind smile and started to pull off. "Of course, Carley. I know you wonder about them, too." She smiled sadly. "I haven't seen them in weeks, but I intend to today."

Chris

It had been a long day again. Lately it had been a harder and harder struggle to get through the day. She didn't know if it was her age or what, but she was restless. She felt like she should be doing something more with her life. Maybe she needed a good hobby. For the last twelve years she had been so busy being a mom and wife that she had forgotten how to just be herself. Lord, she didn't even know who Christine Dosser was anymore.

There was a knock on the front door that shook her from her reverie. She didn't recognize the man on the doorstep.

"Hello, Mrs. Dosser?"

"Yes, may I help you?" she asked.

"I am detective Harold McFall with the county social services division. I was hoping to ask you some questions. Do you have a few minutes?" he asked.

Chris was baffled. What in the world? "Of course, sir. Please come in." She moved aside and let him into her living room. She hurried to move Drew's basketball from the couch so that he could sit down. She hoped the house didn't still smell like the bacon she had cooked this morning.

"Mrs. Dosser, I will be brief and to the point. My office has been contacted by an anonymous person about your niece, Katie. There is some concern that she may have been the victim of abuse." Chris gasped and stared speechless at the detective.

"I don't understand. What kind of abuse?" she asked in disbelief. Sure, she hadn't seen Katie in a while but surely she was alright.

"Mrs. Dosser, let me just tell you the basic facts so far. It seems that pretty soon after the adoption, your sister, Ashley, suffered from some sort of medical condition. I don't know yet the specifics on that matter. Regardless,—".

"Wait right there. What adoption?"

"The adoption of Katie by your brother in law Kevin Landers."

"I didn't know he had followed through with that yet. Are you sure?" she asked in disbelief. It seemed like a bad time to be handling legal matters with his wife that sick. Could Ashley even legally sign adoption papers in her condition?

"Yes, ma'am. I have reviewed the paperwork myself. The adoption was finalized over a month ago. It is apparent that since your sister has been sick, Kevin has asked Mrs. Sandra Chalmers to help out more and more with Katie's care. Kevin says that Katie has practically been living with Sandra. Do you know anything about this arrangement?"

"No, I am afraid that I haven't spoken to my sister or Kevin in quite a while. I didn't know that Sandra had been watching Katie. The last time I talked with Ashley, she mentioned that Kevin didn't want Sandra at their home and had cut back on her hours. Can you please tell me what abuse you are investigating?"

"Physical abuse, ma'am. Katie has several bruises on her head, arms and legs. I understand that she suffered a broken arm a few months ago also. Her right arm is apparently fractured again as well. When we interrogated Mr. and Mrs. Landers, it was evident that Mrs. Lander's was in no mental state to accurately answer our questions. We suspect that Mrs. Chalmers has been abusing Katie. She was in Mrs. Chalmer's care the night she broke her arm. Now she has been caring for Katie almost exclusively. Katie has several obvious signs of abuse. This has been going on a while. I am sorry to break this news to you, ma'am. I can see that you are extremely upset."

"For a while? Why didn't someone call sooner? What about at school? Didn't any teacher suspect something?" she grasped for answers and could hear how her voice quavered.

"No, because Katie has been pulled from school. She hasn't been since before Christmas. She was being tutored by Sandra on a home school basis. Mr. Landers states that this was for the child's benefit." Chris didn't know what to say. Sandra had hurt Katie? No way. Sandra loved Katie with all her heart. Oh my, this was going to devastate her. Chris could almost feel Sandra's outrage. She didn't know what was going on here, but she didn't believe that Sandra had hurt Katie. There had to be another answer.

"Have you ever witnessed Mrs. Chalmers doing anything that could be construed as abuse? Was Katie scared of her? Was she demanding and dominating? What about just a little bit too sweet to Katie? Did you ever see any bruises on Katie? Have you seen Mrs. Chalmers and Katie together in the last two months?"

The list went on and on. Chris answered all the questions as honestly as she could.

"Thank you so much for your willingness to help us with this case, Mrs. Dosser. We will be in touch."

As he was turning to go out the door to leave, Carley ran up the steps of the house and almost slid into the detective. She stopped in surprise when she saw the badge on his belt loop.

"Oh my goodness, you already know. Thank goodness!" She exclaimed in delight. Chris inhaled in surprise and asked, "Carley what in the world do you mean? We know what?"

"About Katie. Oh, thank you. Thank you. Mom, she looks so bad. She is bruised and looks so frightened. I just saw Sandra headed that way!" Chris and the detective's eyes met in silent acknowledgement. He pulled his cell phone from his pocket and made the call.

Sandra

Looked like no one was home. The car was in the yard but no one came to the door. She was about to turn around and leave when she heard a noise inside. Was that yelling? She pressed her ear up to the door and listened again. The wind had picked up this morning so it was hard to tell. Probably just the wind, she thought. Again, she turned to go. She heard a frantic barking coming from inside the door. Rosie! Sandra had wondered how the little dog was doing. From up in the second story Sandra clearly heard the sound of Katie screaming. Sandra thought her heart would stop on the spot she was so scared. What in the world would she do? She looked around frantically for help but of course this far from town, no one was around.

"Katie?" she yelled. She backed up to look up at the window to Katie's room. Rosie continued to whimper and scratch on the door. She felt a sense of urgency. She had to go help Katie. With a moment's thought, she looked around, trying to spot something to use to get the door open. A few feet to the right of the porch, she saw a rusted piece of iron leaning up against the concrete. With both hands she grasped the metal and ran back to the front door with her heart racing. It took three sharp blows, but eventually the door knob came loose. She threw the door open and yelled up to Katie. When she didn't get an answer, she started up the stairs. She couldn't help but notice the smell of the place. Smelled like a garbage dump already. Dirty dishes and clothes were everywhere. Newspapers had been put down for Rosie but never cleaned up. The smell of dog urine was overwhelming.

She met Kevin coming down the stairs and almost fell back down. She retreated back down to the ground floor and watched him. He seemed just as shocked to see her. She noticed the smell of alcohol immediately. It hung around him like a cloud. His bloodshot eyes pored over her and he smiled a treacherous smile. Sandra felt her blood run cold. No backing out now old girl, she chided herself. "Where is Katie? Kevin, do you hear me? What is wrong with Katie? I heard her yelling."

"Nothing is wrong with that kid except she needs to be taught some manners. She took something she shouldn't have and I had to discipline her. She is fine. I was made to mind when I was little and look how I turned out." With that he tilted his head back and laughed so loud and long that Sandra thought for sure he had lost what little mind he had left.

"Sandra? Is that you?" a little voice said from the top of the stairs.

"Katie, are you okay? Sandra is going to get you out of here sweetie." She struggled to see around him to inspect Katie, but Kevin blocked her view. "Don't you worry, honey. Kevin, I am going to call the authorities. Ashley evidently is in worse shape than I expected to allow this to happen. She needs medical attention and so does Katie and I intent for that to start right now."

She pushed around Kevin and jerked away when he grabbed her by the arm. "Don't you touch me, you rotten, no good coward. You may have hurt that child, and you have hurt Ashley, too. But you will not touch me. Get your hands off of me!" she shouted. She looked shocked when the pistol went off. She sank to her knees and held her chest for just a moment before falling flat on her face onto the hardwood floor. The rusted piece of iron clattered loudly against the hardwood floor. Blood immediately created a circle around her body. Katie was screaming. Katie was screaming and screaming and screaming.

Kevin

That couldn't have been better choreographed if he were a director on a movie set. The police cruisers came flying into the driveway about the time he shot Sandra. Ashley, awakened from her stupor by the chaos, stumbled down the stairs and slipped in Sandra's blood. Kevin didn't even have to think. He just handed the pistol to Ashley and stepped away. The police officers rushed through the still open door and saw Ashley covered in blood and holding the pistol.

Ashley had had the shell shocked look of a war veteran. Her eyes were glazed over. She collapsed on the floor and started to moan in the most inhuman sound Kevin had ever heard. She rocked back and forth and didn't seem to hear Katie crying upstairs or the policemen shouting at her to lay the pistol down. Two of the officers had drawn their own weapons and were pointing them at her. Kevin raised his hands to be sure he wasn't seen as a threat.

"Oh, thank God you are here. Oh thank you, thank you. I don't know what just happened. It all happened so fast. Ashley, honey, please lay that pistol down. Please, honey. It's over. She is dead. She can't hurt Katie anymore." He allowed his voice to crack and his eyes to tear up. Ashley glanced over her shoulder at Kevin and seemed to finally understand what had happened. She looked down her arm at the hand that held the pistol and then she looked down at her legs which were covered in drying blood. Suddenly she threw the pistol down like it was on fire. The officers flinched and then one ran to grab the gun while the other helped her to her feet.

"Ma'am? Can you tell me what happened?" An officer bent over Sandra and felt her neck for a pulse. After a moment he looked up and shook his head. Outside the sound of sirens approaching caught everyone's attention. Paramedics rushed into the room and immediately started to work on Sandra. One lady looked over Ashley's bloodied body with concern.

"She's okay. It's that lady I am worried about," Kevin said pointing to Sandra.

"I didn't do it." Ashley's voice seemed to come from someone else's mouth.

"Honey. It's okay. You came in and saw Sandra hitting Katie again and you had to stop her. It's okay." He gently put his arms around her and stroked her hair. She pushed him away and tried to stand.

"Katie?" she called.

Katie

Rosie's fur was soft. Katie didn't even smile when Rosie licked her face and whined. It was not real. Mom said nightmares weren't real. This was just a nightmare like that one about the dragon and in just a minute she would wake up. The carpet was rough and left marks on her cheek. It was a little bit itchy too. Maybe when she woke up Kevin would have been a dream too. All that would be real is her and Mommy and Rosie. Things would be back like they used to be when everything was good and happy.

From a distance she heard something she hadn't heard in a while. Was that really Mommy calling her name or was that a part of her nightmare, too? It was so hard to tell. No, there it was again and her voice was closer than before. Better just wait and see. Didn't want to come out and find Kevin waiting for her. Her face hurt. Kevin had been really mad when he couldn't find Mom's medicine. He had started throwing things around and screaming bad words. Finally he had come up the stairs and found Katie hiding in the closet. Now her cheek hurt worse than her arm did, she had whelps on her back, and she was tired of being scared.

"Katie?" Mommy was in her room now. Katie peeked out from under her bed to see if it was really real. Sure enough there she was. She didn't look good at all, but it was her mom. Katie crawled out and stood to hug her mom. That was when she noticed blood all over her legs.

"Mom?" she cried in alarm. "Sandra didn't really get hurt did she? It was just a dream right? Kevin didn't shoot her with that gun right?"

Mommy just sank down onto the floor and held Katie close. Katie let herself be calmed and comforted in her Mommy's arms. It had been so long since she had felt safe.

Chris

Chris got the car in drive and headed out of the driveway without really knowing what she was doing. It took her a minute to see that Carley had jumped into the passenger seat and was riding along. "Mom? Are you okay? What did I say? Where are we going?"

"Carley, that detective was at our house because Sandra has been accused of hurting Katie. He was trying to find out if it were true or not. When you came in and said that you had seen Sandra heading out to Ashley's, we knew it may have been true after all. Sandra has been telling everyone that she hasn't been there in a while but you saw her yourself, so evidently she has been lying. Gosh, Carley, I had no idea. None. I feel so stupid for not seeing."

"Mom, something is wrong. I went to Ashley's today." She flinched in anticipation of her mom's outrage. When she remained calm, Carley continued. "I'm sorry for not telling you I was going, but I was afraid you would stop me and I really wanted to see Katie. Kevin was there and I swear Katie is scared to death of him. He wouldn't let me see Ashley. He scared me so bad, Mom. I ran out of there and started home and that is where I saw Sandra. She said she was on her way to Ashley's." Carley began to cry.

They pulled up in the driveway just in time to see paramedics carrying a stretcher to the awaiting ambulance. The figure on the stretcher was covered from head to toe with a blanket. Chris almost panicked when she saw the coroner's car parked next to the ambulance. She jumped out of the car almost before she had put it in park and began to run up the sidewalk to the house. She was met by two uniformed police officer's who grabbed her and made her stop.

"Where is my sister? I am Ashley's sister. Is she okay? Where is Katie?"

"Madam, please stop. This is a crime scene and we can't let you in there. I believe Mrs. Landers is in the back yard with her daughter." Chris didn't wait to be invited. She ran as fast as she could into the back yard to find her sister. She found her sitting in the swing holding Katie close to her. When Ashley saw Chris she stared. It had been so long since she had seen her and she still didn't know what to make of Chris and Kevin. Chris couldn't take her eyes off Ashley. She looked so thin and scared. Her hair hung in strands around her face and it was obvious she had been crying. Her eyes looked so dark and were sunk way back in her head. All thoughts of hate she had had for Ashley left. It no longer mattered what had happened before. All she knew was that her sister and best friend needed her.

"Ashley! What happened?" She ran to her and took her in her arms. "Ashley, I am so sorry for not being here for you. Are you okay? What happened?" Ashley's eyes seemed vacant and confused.

"I didn't do it." she said again.

"You didn't do what? What is going on around here? Who is on that stretcher?"

About that time Kevin walked around the side of the house with an investigator. She heard him saying, "Yeah and then I heard a blast and ran back into the room to see Ashley holding a pistol. Sandra was on the floor and blood was already starting to pool under her. Katie was screaming. It was hell. Utter hell. I don't even know where she got the pistol. I never believed in keeping firearms in the house."

Kevin looked up and saw Chris standing in his back yard with Ashley.

"Hello, Chris. Good to see you again. Glad you could finally make it." With that he turned and went back out front with the officer in tow.

Chris looked down at Katie. She seemed to be in shock. When she lowered her arms Katie willingly went into them for a hug from her aunt.

"I thought you didn't love me anymore, Aunt Chris. Are you mad at me?" Chris' heart broke at that statement. What had she been avoiding here? Obviously things had been terrible. She felt remorse for not coming out sooner and talking with Ashley.

"I didn't do it." Ashley said again. "I didn't do it."

Two officers approached them and one quietly spoke to Ashley. "Mrs. Landers, you have the right to remain silent." Chris didn't remember much more after that. She knew that she had taken Katie when she had started to scream. All Ashley had said was, "I didn't do it."

Carley

This was a nightmare. Sandra was dead? She had been accused of hurting Katie? She didn't believe it. Not one word of it. It had been Kevin and she knew that as well as she knew her own name. No one else had seen the look on his face or how Katie had reacted to him. No one had seen the look of concern on Sandra's face either. Carley knew that Sandra had meant to go there because she was worried about Katie, just as she had been. Now Sandra was dead and it was her fault. She shouldn't have opened her big mouth. If she had kept quiet things would have been different.

Ashley

She thought that about two days had passed since she had been taken to jail. She was starting to feel more clear-headed. Of course, Kevin hadn't been here to give her that medication, either. He had been so mad the other day when he couldn't find the bottle. It was the day Sandra had been shot. Ashley held her head in her hands. Oh, God. Sweet Sandra was dead and she had been accused of killing her. How was she going to make everyone believe her? She was being held in the mental facility because Kevin had told them she was on drugs and had been treated by a psychiatrist. She didn't remember going to see any psychiatrist, but who knows what she didn't remember. The last month had been a blur of medicine and sleep. She wanted to go home to check on Katie. She had to get out of here or she would go crazy-for real this time.

Kevin

It had been quiet at the house without Ashley. Too bad about Sandra. He had tried and tried to tell Sandra to stay away, but the busybody wouldn't listen. He took another drink from his bottle and thought about how to handle all of this. He wanted Ashley with him. He loved her so much. She was his. He had tried to post bond yesterday, but the officials said she needed further treatment before she was in any shape to go home. Go figure. First he was crazy and now his wife. Oh well, two of a feather and all that.

When he had found the pistol under her journal in the bedside table, he had been shocked. Why would she feel like she needed a weapon? He was here to protect her from anything that scared her. The police officers had discovered that she had bought it at a pawn shop on the edge of town several weeks ago. That discovery added to the idea that Sandra's murder was premeditated. No one seemed to suspect that she hadn't killed Sandra. Who was going to believe a woman who was being treated for depression by a psychiatrist? He knew that the good doctor would be happy to say that she had been clinically depressed to the point of suicide for weeks now. He would even produce copies of prescriptions, if needed. He had been treating her with some very powerful medications to combat the depression. That medication still hadn't been found. Kevin knew that Katie had done something with it. He had done everything he knew to do to get her to tell him where it was. Stubborn little girl. Well, she would learn soon that it didn't pay to go against him. All she needed was a father's firm hand.

Sometimes the best thing to do when things got too sticky was to pull up stakes and move on. It would be hard to leave his beautiful house but there were more houses all over the country waiting for him to restore them. Actually, he thought, it would be a shame to stay here. There were so many places he wanted to share with Ashley and Katie. Yes, he decided. We will move on just as soon as Ashley was cleared. He needed to be able to think clearly. Abruptly he stood up and went into the kitchen and poured the bottle of whiskey down the drain. He looked around the place. What a mess! No wonder the cops had looked around in disgust. "Katie! Get down here sweetheart. You and I have some cleaning up to do." Hours later he was satisfied at the amount of work they had accomplished. The house smelled nice and clean. Now he needed to contact his lawyer. Ashley had killed Sandra out of self-defense. He needed someone who could prove that. He picked up the phone and made a call.

Katie

"That's a good girl, Rosie. You just lie still and be a good girl. I will brush your hair and make you look so pretty. You and I have to look good today. We are going to go see Mommy. Daddy said so." She was so glad that Daddy was feeling better. He didn't smell like he usually did and he seemed happy. But she missed her though!

Dad said that she had to go back to school in the morning. Katie was secretly happy about that. She was bored at home with nothing to do. Kevin had said that he wanted her to start calling him Daddy, so that was what she was doing. Didn't want to give him any reason to be mad at her. Daddy said that she was a good girl and he was going to buy her something new. She wondered what it would be. Maybe some new clothes or a new doll. She hadn't gotten anything for Christmas. Katie figured it was because she hadn't helped Mom. Santa must have known that she hadn't.

Some people had come to the house and asked her a bunch of questions about Sandra. She had been so careful to tell them exactly what Daddy had told her to even though she thought it was lying. Mommy had always punished her for lying before but now it must be okay. Daddy had lied to people too. He said that all of these strangers wanted to take her away to go live somewhere else. If she didn't tell them exactly what he told her to they would take her away forever and she would never see Mom again.

She had heard him tell them that Mommy had hurt Sandra, but she had seen him do it. Of course, she couldn't tell anybody about that, ever. Daddy had told her over and over again what would happen if anyone ever found out.

Sometimes her head hurt from trying to keep it all straight. She was a little bit worried about going to school because people there might know what had happened. She bet nobody else in her class had ever seen so much blood before. This thought made her scared so she jumped up and went downstairs.

Daddy was on the phone.

Chris

It was so hard to believe all that had happened. Sandra's family was outraged at the accusations being made against her. Sandra's daughter said that red velvet cupcakes had been in her mother's car. Obviously, Sandra had been intending to give them to Katie. Everybody knew how much Katie loved red velvet cupcakes. Why would a woman who was abusing a little girl take the time to make her favorite dessert?

The detective had told Chris that Katie had confirmed the abuse. He said that the case was closed because Katie had identified Sandra as her abuser. Chris hadn't been able to sleep since she had heard this. All these years and no one had known about it. How had she gotten by with it all these years? Or had she just started it? Who knew? Ashley may have some answers but her doctor had made sure that everyone left her alone. He said that she was too emotionally unstable to be defending her actions right now. If all of this was true, then Chris believed that she deserved a medal for killing her.

The defense attorney was planning to use self-defense to get Ashley off the murder charge. Chris figured that surely any one on the jury would agree. Anyone who walked in and saw a person hurting a child would surely have acted the same. She had to admit that as far as legal things went she was clueless. She only hoped that Kevin hired a good attorney. Goodness knows that Ashley needed all the help she could get.

Daniel

The day went from good to bad and then from bad to worse. He got into work late because Drew couldn't find his football jersey. They had looked everywhere except in his backpack where Chris had put it. Finally he had called her at work and she had told him where it was and implied that he didn't know anything about the family. This settled, he had rushed into work fifteen minutes late and saw his boss leaned up against his desk waiting for him. This couldn't be good. Not only did he know Daniel was late, but he saw the mess Daniel had left behind last night as well. He couldn't seem to keep up with the paperwork.

"Daniel, what's up, my man?" Mr. Reeves said jovially. Daniel knew this was a bad sign. Mr. Reeves was never in a good mood this early in the morning.

"Sorry to be late, boss. Won't happen again." He realized that he sounded like a seventeen year old on his first job, but he didn't know how else to be.

"Oh, no problem, Daniel. I just thought I would stop by and personally see how things are going with you in the eastern district. Got a call from Marck yesterday. Seems like your sell of the new decongestant is down. They put a little pressure on, you know. Don't want them to start looking elsewhere. Anything wrong?" His piercing look belied any good intention and Daniel knew his ass was on the line. Got to make it good or else.

"No, no. Just hit a snag at that new medical building out on Parkway. Doctors out of town on vacation, you know how it is. I'm sure my ratio will be right back up next week."

"Oh, good. Wouldn't want to have to embarrass you." He laughed and made his way out the door, where he turned and issued the ultimatum. "We'll have lunch next Friday just to go over some numbers, Daniel. One o'clock at Finley's."

Daniel sank down in his chair and inhaled a deep breath. This was it. One week. There was no way he could pull into ranks in one week and Mr. Reeve knew it. He was only giving him time because he hadn't decided who to put in Daniel's position yet. Oh, God. How was he going to tell Chris that he hadn't made it? With all that she had had to endure lately, he feared that this would be the final straw.

Kevin

Money talks! That big-time attorney from the Atlanta law firm had managed to get Ashley release on bail. He had called to say that Ashley was free to come home. Kevin had to post a half-million dollar bond, but it was no problem for him. She was a special girl. If she was good, she could hope for a clean slate of innocence of the charges. They were going for self-defense. The lawyer had been so sure that this would work. He'd better be right. Kevin wanted Ashley off the hook and when he wanted something, he usually got it. He took one more look in the mirror and was happy with what he saw. He looked young and fresh. He wanted to look his best for his bride. She was a good one and he wanted to make her happy.

He yelled up at Katie to come on downstairs. She was a pretty little girl. He had bought her a new dress to wear today and it looked adorable on her. He knew that Ashley would appreciate him thinking of her. He wondered if she knew about the adoption. Chris had a big mouth and he didn't know how much time she had spent with Ashley in the backyard before he had came back there. Of course, Ashley hadn't been up to par that day either.

He was a little bit worried about her state of mind now. She was no longer on the medication, and he didn't know how much she actually remembered. It didn't really matter because he knew that she loved him and would do whatever he asked. She worshipped him. It was obvious when she looked at him how much she loved him.

Ashley

She didn't think that Katie had ever looked prettier. She had on a new pink dress with new Mary Jane slippers. Kevin had obviously tried to fix her hair in pigtails. One pigtail was higher than the other, but she knew that Katie had to be the most beautiful child in the world. When Katie smiled, she lit up the world. Katie turned that smile on her mother and Ashley fell in love with her all over again. She ran as fast as she could to embrace her daughter. This was the longest she had ever been away from her. She had been absent for longer than this if you considered all the days she had been confined to the bed at home.

Next, she turned to Kevin. He was looking at her as if he hadn't ever done a thing to hurt her. How could someone be two different people? If she tried to put the last few weeks out of her mind she could easily just slip back into loving him. He looked at her with such awe and love in his eyes that to anyone else he would seem like a devoted husband and father. Her eyes turned to slits and the look of hate on her face stopped him in his tracks. To an outsider the scenario may have seemed almost comical. The way she just had to level a stare at him and he immediately halted and looked at her in disbelief.

"Don't take one more step towards me or my daughter," she demanded. Kevin couldn't seem to fathom any reason she would be speaking to him in such a manner.

"Ashley? Dear, what is wrong? Aren't you happy to see us? We came to bring you home."

"I said stop and I mean it, Kevin Landers." Her tone of voice caused two uniformed officers behind the desk to stop what they were doing and stare in concern. Kevin hadn't let this go by unnoticed. He glanced out of the corner of his eye to see how much time he had. Ashley could see the calculated look in his eyes she recognized from times before when he had been up to something devious. She briskly took Katie and started to walk out of the building. She knew better than to cause any more trouble. She was lucky to be leaving to start with. She couldn't do anything to land her back in jail.

On the ride home she sat in silence. Kevin kept glancing over at her but he kept his mouth shut. She asked him to stop at the local market with the excuse that she needed a few things. "I'll just be a minute. Please just stay in the car with Katie. It's so cold and I don't want her to have to get out for just this few minutes. Just keep the engine and heat running. Anything you need?" she asked. This seemed to appease him a little bit. For once he obliged without argument. Usually he was right there wherever she went like he was afraid she would vanish or something.

She almost ran into the store. All eyes were on her as she entered the store. After all, she was the murderer of a local woman whom everyone loved dearly. Never mind the alleged abuse; no one believed a word of that garbage. Ashley knew how they felt. She didn't believe any of this either. She made her way over to the pharmacy and pretended to search for something she needed until the whispers faded and some semblance of normalcy began. Quietly she slipped into an office in the back of the store and shut the door. She grabbed the phone from the desk and dialed Chris' number as quickly as she could.

"Please be home. Please be home," she whispered.

"Hello?" Ashley was so relieved to hear her sister's voice that she almost lost her nerve. She exhaled her held breath and almost sobbed in desperation. "Chris, I am out of jail. I am going home to act like normal. Something is bad wrong. I didn't kill Sandra, Kevin did. He put the gun in my hand. He has been drugging me. He has the doctor under his thumb." At Chris' startled gasp, she hurried on.

"Listen very carefully, Chris. I don't have much time. I will be fine for a while. Find out anything you can about him and his past. Find out if Sandra knew something she shouldn't have. Do it now."

With this, she carefully laid the phone back on the receiver and took her first full breath. She knew that Chris could be trusted to do whatever was necessary without any further direction.

"Please, God. Help me get my Katie out of this mess," she prayed.

Carley

Sometimes she just came here to sit and think. She didn't tell anybody because they would say she was morbid and weird. While all her friends were thinking about tests and boys and music she was living with the knowledge that she had caused sweet Sandra to get killed. Her mom and dad had made sure to talk to her about it and assure her that this wasn't true, but Carley knew better. She wasn't a kid anymore and she knew how the world worked. She just wished that she could go back and relive that day when she had met Sandra on the road. What would have happened if she had gotten into the car and gone with Sandra? What if she had simply told Sandra that she was just coming from there and that Kevin was crazy? Sandra would have believed her and went with her to talk to the police or Carley's parents or something. Sandra would have known what to do.

Why hadn't she done the right thing? Sighing deeply, she gazed up at Sandra's back porch door. This old swing was just about to fall, but Carley felt some comfort when sitting here where Sandra had spent so much time. She knew that soon Sandra's family would come and sort out her belongings and this place would probably be sold. This thought made her sorrowful. She was drying her tears a while later when she heard a car pull into the driveway around front. Who was here? She got up and crept around the side of the house to see. Carley didn't know her heart could beat as hard as it did when she saw her mother walking up the sidewalk. Oh boy. Here we go. She would be in big trouble for being here instead of at the library where she was supposed to be.

"Mom? I'm so sorry." Chris seemed to almost jump out of her skin.

"Carley? What in the world are you doing here?" she asked in amazement. Carley didn't think she had ever seen such a look on her mom's face before. She looked guilty.

"Mom? What's wrong? Something is up. You didn't even know I was here, did you?" she asked. She felt like the roles were reversed and she was the one asking the questions for a change. Not a bad feeling, either.

Chris seemed to weigh the options before speaking. After a moment she decided to let Carley in on her plan. "Carley, I may need your help. Ashley is out of jail. She called me and asked me to find out if Sandra knew something about Kevin that he didn't want her to know. She said that he killed Sandra, not her."

Carley could believe this after seeing his face and now finally someone else did too.

"What are we going to do?" she asked with no hesitation. Chris seemed to wonder for the first time why Carley had been here in the first place. The lack of hesitation made her wonder if Carley had suspected this all along. Maybe she had misjudged her daughter.

"We are going to break and enter, my darling. Not my finest parenting but right now I have to know if Sandra suspected Kevin of something. I think maybe we should go in the back door so no one notices us." Carley tapped Chris on the shoulder and pointed at the car in the driveway.

"Um, Mom, I think the car is a dead giveaway. Look, I'll sit right here on the steps and look sad. If someone comes over I will call for you. Kind of like a lookout. You go in and look around. Look in hidden places. Sandra wouldn't have left anything lying out in the open."

Chris

Chris stared at Carley, and then turned and did as instructed. The back door wasn't locked. She went into the kitchen and looked around. How could it still smell like cake in here? The smell made her think about Sandra and all she had done to help out with Katie since she had been born. Chris missed her so much. She had been part of their family. She would come into the salon and announce that she was going to do something different and drastic with her hair. She was ready to go wild. Then, when she would describe what she wanted, Chris would just try to hide her smile. She always went right back to the exact same style she had had for twenty plus years. Chris would smile, agree, do as Sandra had asked, and praise her for being bold and daring.

Her shawl was still hanging over the back of one of the dining room chairs. Chris reached and ran her hand over the soft hand knit fabric. "We miss you, Sandra. Sorry to intrude, but I have to help Ashley. I am sure you wouldn't mind," she said aloud to an empty house. When she got to the bedroom she stopped and looked around. She had never been to this part of the house before. Pictures of Sandra and her husband on their wedding day graced the top of her dresser. A strand of pearls lay next to a bronzed pair of baby shoes. Everything was neat and clean and orderly as expected. Sandra wasn't one for nonsense.

What could she have possibly known about Kevin? Maybe she had run across some kind of paperwork or heard a private phone call. Maybe she had witnessed him hurting Katie or Ashley. All of these possibilities were not the kind of thing that left a trail. Where to look? She looked under the bed and found nothing. A quick look in the dresser drawers revealed nothing as well. Chris about jumped a mile when she heard footsteps behind her. Carley appeared looking worried.

"Mom, what's taking so long? I'm afraid somebody is going to notice your car. Did you look in here?" She opened the closet door and rummaged around the back wall. In a second a little door opened and Carley reached into the opening and produced an envelope of papers.

169

"How did you know about that door?" Chris asked in amazement.

"One day Katie and I came home with Sandra and we played in here. We found it and asked Sandra about it. She laughed and said that it was her hiding spot."

Chris didn't know who was more nervous, her or Carley. Carley had talked her into opening the envelope to just see if it was anything pertaining to Kevin. It seemed like some sort of legal document with Kevin Lander's name on top. This was all she needed to know. She stuck the envelope in her pocket and hurried out the door. She needed privacy and time to process this information.

On the ride home, Carley was strangely talkative. Maybe she liked being involved in things. She wasn't a little girl anymore. Chris wondered what else she had missed about her daughter. She hadn't known how inquisitive she was or how outgoing. She hadn't even hesitated to help out and had needed no direction.

"Carley I don't know how all of this is going to turn out. I don't know what these papers are, but I figure that Sandra wouldn't have taken them if they hadn't been important. I really appreciate your help and I have to admit that I haven't been myself lately. Things have been so messed up. First Daddy gets a new job and is gone all the time, and then Ashley gets married to a stranger. Then Daddy and I were fighting there for a while. Now Sandra is dead and your aunt Ashley is accused of shooting her for abusing Katie. I know this seems like too much, but I promise that this will be resolved soon. I hope you will forgive me for being so inattentive. I have done you a disfavor by letting you just coast through these things with no explanation. I promise from now on to be better. I'm sorry."

"Mom. Can I ask you for a favor?" Carley looked sideways at her mom for the answer, expecting something that she couldn't promise.

"Of course, honey."

"I want to take art classes instead of band and chorus. I really love drawing and painting a lot more than I do those things. Would you be disappointed in me?"

Chris was baffled by this sudden change in subject. Art? She had had no idea her daughter liked art. Had she ever told her that before or had she simply kept quiet and did what she thought her mom wanted her to do?

"Carley, I am so proud of you for telling me this. I would love for you to do whatever you feel like you would excel in, honey. If its art that you love, then its art you shall do. Is the school offering classes or do we need to check around?" she asked optimistically. Her mission was temporarily put on hold as she learned a new aspect of her daughter.

Daniel

Well, today was the day. He had lost his job to a twenty four year old, college-educated brat. To make matters worse, today was his birthday. Too bad he didn't even feel like stopping at the bar for a beer. He needed two. One to cry in and one to toast to being forty. Forty. How would he ever find a new job at this age? It had been pure luck when he landed this one and he couldn't even do the work. Chris would be so disappointed in him. She had a lot on her shoulders right now. Ashley was in jail and he honestly didn't know what would happen to her.

He turned into the driveway and got out of the car just as Kevin pulled up into the driveway. Daniel was surprised to see him.

"Hey, buddy. Good to see ya, come on it." He greeted Kevin warmly, and led him to sit on the sofa by the fire, then went into the kitchen for beers.

"What's up? You doing okay? Seems a little early for you to be off work. Everything alright?" Daniel just nodded and drank deeply of his beer. Needed a minute to relax before admitting to his failure.

"Yeah, fine. You ok?"

"Oh, yeah. Making it fine. Hey, I've been meaning to ask you something for a while. Didn't get to be really sociable last time you came over. Ashley wasn't in great shape you know? Anyway, I've been wondering what kind of drugs you have access to. What do you peddle?" Daniel was a little bit worried about this question. What kind of drugs did he need?

"Oh, you know. Antibiotics, birth control, etc. What you in the market for, friend?" He laughed to lighten the mood. Surely Kevin was joking anyway. He eyed Kevin a little suspiciously. Kevin seemed to sense Daniels apprehension and changed the subject.

"You know that Ashley got to come home today, huh?"

Daniel jumped up and almost spilled his beer. "Oh, that is so great! Your attorney must have done a wonderful job!"

"Yes, he is good. But to tell you the truth, Daniel, something isn't right with her. She won't talk to me. I sure hope her depression isn't coming back. Those imbeciles at the jail took her off her medication. She went right up to bed and took Katie with her. I need someone to talk to. I'm worried. I got her out on bond, but I don't know if I can keep her out of jail. I mean, this is murder. People don't normally walk away from those kinds of charges."

Daniel rubbed his eyes with the heels of his hands and agreed. "I know what you mean. Chris seems to think that she will just saunter up to the judge and bat her pretty eyes and he will feel sorry for her and let her off the hook. That's not reality. I take it that your lawyer has a lot of experience in things like this?"

"He's supposed to be the best. Came up from Atlanta. Guy by the name of Alan Guthrie. Heard of him?"
"No, but I don't socialize with those liars." They both chuckled at the joke.

"So how is Katie holding up?"

"She is just fine. You know kids. They forget stuff just as fast as they witness it. She probably doesn't even remember."

Daniel was puzzled by this statement and he studied Kevin's face for clues that he was joking. Any idiot knew better than that.

Ashley

It was good to be back with Katie. She had been so worried while in jail that Kevin might hurt her or at the least just ignore her. More and more of the past weeks were surfacing in her memory. Had he really hit Katie? What kind of drugs did he give her that honestly made her unable to respond to her daughter's cries? Tears escaped her eye lids and she moved a little bit closer to her sleeping little girl. Katie reached out in her sleep and grasped Ashley's hand. Oh, Lord, how was she supposed to get out of this mess? Murder? Dear God. She had not killed Sandra and it almost broke her heart to realize that any person in their right mind would even believe for a minute that she had. Surely nobody believed that Sandra had hurt Katie. Sandra had loved this child almost as much as Ashley did. She continued to cry into her pillow. She didn't want Kevin to come in here and ask questions. She had decided for now to just let him think she was traumatized and depressed. Maybe he would leave her alone if he thought she was bed bound.

She needed to talk to Chris. Chris had always known what to do. In all her life she couldn't remember a moment when Chris hadn't had her act together. If something puzzled her she just figured it out. Ashley knew that Chris would help her get to the bottom of this. Darn, but she needed her cell phone. She never had found it after that night that Kevin had come to Chris'. Afterwards he had insisted that she didn't need one. Now she did. She couldn't very well use the phone in the den where Kevin could listen to her conversation. She wondered what he would say if she said she wanted to go see Chris.

If she was correct in her thinking, he had lied to her about Chris. He obviously needed a reason for her not to be around Chris and his plan had worked miraculously. Stupid, stupid, stupid! Had she really let him estrange her from her very best friend? She had believed him over her sister. That was incredible—even to her.

It was time to think and make a plan. First thing she needed was to know who he really was. These last few weeks had proven over and over that he wasn't stable. Honestly, she was scared to death of him. He had actually given her drugs to keep her home with him while he abused her and Katie. That thought almost made her scream in rage, but there was no time for that now. For now she would act meek and humble and appreciative of him for helping her. Her time would come for revenge and when it did, God help him.

Katie

Mom was home. She had been home for a week now but things still didn't feel normal. Mom seemed like she was acting. She wasn't acting when she hugged and kissed Katie and told her how much she loved her. She was acting when she did these things to Kevin. Katie had asked Mom about this, but Mom had shushed her and asked her to be quiet.

Rosie was growing up so big and strong. She still followed Katie everywhere and now she even knew some tricks. Katie was practicing fetch with her now. It was cold and a little bit rainy outside, but she didn't care. She wanted to be out away from Mom and Dad. They seemed to think that she couldn't hear them, but she could. Just because she was a kid didn't mean that she didn't understand what they were saying. Some people thought that Mom had hurt Sandra and they wanted Mom to stay in jail forever. Katie cried when she thought about this.

Even though Daddy acted funny now, he hadn't hurt her since Mommy had been home. When she got in trouble now, he let her go to her room. He didn't spank her or slap her anymore. Katie thought that Mom might know about how he had done this before but she wasn't sure. She wasn't going to ask her either. He wasn't as mean when he wasn't drinking that stuff that smelled so bad.

She heard the sound of Mom and Dad talking in the kitchen. She moved a little bit closer to the window so she could hear better. "You know as well as I do that Daniel wouldn't come over here if Chris had told him about what happened between you and her. I am sure that she is sorry and embarrassed. She must have just went a little bit crazy for a minute. Please, let me go see her. I want to talk to her for a little while. You know that I might be going back to jail soon. I need to talk to my sister and see my niece and nephew. You can come too. I just need to forgive her, darling. Please?"

Katie didn't like hearing her mom ask permission for anything from Daddy. She was an adult and adults were supposed to make rules. It made her mad. Never before had Mom had to ask to go see Chris. They visited all the time. Mom and Dad kept on talking, but Katie didn't care what else they said. She was tired.

Chris

This was a matter for the police. After reading the paperwork she had gotten from Sandra's house, she realized how much trouble Ashley was in. Why hadn't Sandra said something? Chris wondered how long Sandra had known. It was obvious that Kevin wasn't just a misguided, devious man but an unstable mental patient.

How was she going to get this information to Ashley? She couldn't very well go over there armed with all of this and quietly talk to her and Kevin about it. What would Kevin do if he knew his cover was blown? She needed help. Several days had passed and she still didn't know what to do. She couldn't sleep, thinking about her sister and niece being over there with him. She pulled up in her driveway and was surprised to see Daniel's car in the driveway.

"Daniel? What's wrong, honey. Why are you home at this time of day? They give you an extra half-day off for super sales or something?"

Her excitement turned to fright when she looked him in the eyes and saw the pain reflected there.

"Daniel. What's up? Please talk to me." To her surprise her strong husband sank back into the cushions on the sofa and started to cry. Sob would be a better term to describe it. She had never heard such heart crushing sobs before and momentarily didn't know what to do. She ran to him and took him in her arms. He let himself be held and cried until he could no longer cry. Finally after what seemed like hours, she gently took his chin in her hand and lifted his face to hers. Daniel seemed embarrassed for letting go like that but she wouldn't let him look away.

"I lost my job, Chris. I failed you and Carley and Drew. I thought that I could do it, but I couldn't keep up. I thought I could work my way up and be able to support you so that you could relax a little bit and enjoy life but just like always, I couldn't." This said he started to cry again. Now he seemed more angry than sad. Suddenly he stood up and slammed his fist into the wall.

Chris was scared to move. She had never seen Daniel this upset before. She had had no idea that his job was on the line. Right then and there she realized how distant she had been to her family. She hadn't known how Carley really felt about music. She hadn't known about Daniel's true life. She wondered what major thing she was missing with Drew.

"I'm so sorry I have let you down, Daniel. Please don't apologize for losing your job. I have been so self centered that I have almost lost my family. Maybe not physically but emotionally I have been gone for a while." Daniel looked at her like he couldn't believe she had said that. That quick she had cut to the heart of the matter. Their family had been only acting for so long now. It was time to open up and reveal their true selves to the other.

Daniel seemed to understand where she was coming from. "I let you down. I thought that if I made more money or moved up the corporate ladder maybe you would look at me like you used to. I want you to look at me like I am your world again. I am sorry for letting you down."

Chris couldn't believe that he would think she didn't feel that way about him. She had thought that he knew how much she loved and respected him. She didn't need him to be an executive at a company to please her. She loved him and was proud of who he was. They had a lot to talk about and it seemed like right now was a great time to get started.

Hours later, Chris and Daniel walked hand in hand through their back yard. They had talked about things that they had never been able to talk about before. At was hard to believe that after being together for all these years there were still things she have never told him before. When he had asked her about her father molesting her, she had had to sit down. She didn't know who had told him this lie but she wanted to kill him.

"What? My father was a wonderful man. He never hurt me in any way. He loved Ashley and me until the day he died. Who in the world told you that?" Daniel was taken aback. He had never thought that Kevin might lie about something like that.

"Chris, Kevin told me that the reason Ashley was having mental issues was because your father molested you both. Are you sure that it isn't true? I wouldn't judge you by it, honey." Chris couldn't believe it.

"Daniel, I swear to you that he didn't. Ever. Why would he say that? What possible reason could he have to make you believe that nonsense? Honey, I am seriously concerned about Ashley and I don't mean jail. I did something completely out of character last week and I am embarrassed to tell you about it."

It took her a while to tell him about what she had found at Sandra's house. It was hard to admit that she had involved Carley in her indiscretion but Daniel had only laughed.

"I knew there was more to that girl than meets the eye." Chris laughed. Now that was her old Daniel back again.

"Daniel, you have to help me. Let me show you what I found." She ran into the house and returned with the stack of letters bound by a piece of leather string. "These letters date back three years, Daniel." He pulled one of the letters out of the stack and read it slowly. When his eyes returned to hers she knew that she hadn't overreacted.

Kevin

He was getting tired of playing nursemaid to Ashley. It was time for her to get back to normal. He wanted her to go back to doing laundry and paying bills and even gardening. Maybe she needed a new start. He had started researching property out west and found a quaint little neighborhood in Montana that he would like to see. Yes, that was just what they needed. He would start packing tonight. He felt that time was of the essence. People were nosy in little towns like this. One thing he didn't need at all was some nosy person prying into his business. They didn't need much, just a few clothes and essentials. They could buy all new stuff when they got there. Sometimes this was the best part. When you moved in the middle of the night you got to choose who you would be. A new name, too. Kevin would let Katie pick her own name. He knew that she would get a kick out of that.

Startled from his reverie by the doorbell, he turned and dropped the glass he had been holding. Damn! Another mess to clean up. One thing that wouldn't be going with them was that stupid dog. Chewed up his sock last night. He hurried to the door and looked out the window. Didn't have many visitors anymore. Daniel and Chris were standing out there in the cold. What could they want? Trouble, probably.

"Hey, strangers! Come in, come in. Good to see ya'll. I'll go get Ashley. Maybe a visit from you will cheer her up." They followed him into the den. Ashley appeared moments later with Katie in tow. No one noticed the quick nod from Chris to Ashley that conveyed what she needed to know. Daniel put his feet up on the coffee table and leaned back like he planned to stay a while. Just when he decided to start packing they show up and act like they own the place. Oh well. One last time that they would have to endure them and then they would be history. This made him smile.

Time to move on.

Chris

Daniel was doing a great job of acting normal and drinking beer with Kevin. She quietly excused herself and slipped out of the den. Ashley soon followed with the excuse of getting drinks for them too.

It took her less than a minute to tell Ashley the vital parts of the information she needed and then they went to the kitchen for a glass of water. Chris talked in a loud voice about a customer at the salon so that Ashley could give herself a moment for composure. She had gone over to the stove and stood with her hands over her eyes for a minute. Then, resolved, she had stood up straight and grabbed her sister's hand and strolled back into the den.

When they returned to the den both men were deep in conversation about Sunday's football game. Daniel gave Chris a sidelong glance to see if all was well. Katie was playing quietly in the floor with Rosie. Ashley seemed a little bit quieter after learning the information Chris had brought. Now at least she knew what she was up against and God willing, she would know what to do.

Ashley

Long after everyone else was asleep that night she sat on the bed, waiting. She picked up the phone on the first ring and listened for any indication that Kevin had been awakened. Relief washed over her when she heard him snoring in the other room. All that drinking had left him out for good. She hoped.

"Hello?" she whispered.

"Ashley, you have to listen to me, and listen good. He is dangerous. You have to take Katie and get out of there now. Don't pack anything. Just pick her up and go outside. Chris is waiting in the driveway for you now."

The sound of humming told her that the caller had hung up. She started to tremble in fear. How would she get up enough courage to wake up Katie and carry her outside without waking him up? She took a deep breath and thought for a minute about what the consequences might be. She heard Katie rustle in the bed behind her and was surprised when Katie leaned forward and whispered. "It's okay, Mommy. He won't wake up. I put some of those pills he was giving you in his drink."

Never in her life had she been more astounded. Katie had known about this and planned on him needing to be asleep? She took her little genius in her arms and stood up and started down the stairs.

"Who was that on the phone, Mommy?" She whispered right into Ashley's ear.

"It was your daddy," Ashley whispered back.

Chris

Chris was about ready to call in the police regardless of what anyone else said when she saw Ashley emerge from the house carrying Katie. She ran to them and took Katie from Ashley and placed her in the back seat of the car. Quickly she backed out of the driveway and sped off. Relief washed over her when they were safely away from that monster.

"He will be here in a few hours," she said. Ashley leaned her head back on the headrest and exhaled slowly.

Brad. All these years he had been writing to her and Katie and she hadn't known it. How many hours had she spent being disappointed and hurt because of him and how he left? She had so much to talk to him about. But for now she had to concentrate on getting to somewhere safe from Kevin.

"Where should we go? Daniel is gone to the airport to pick up Brad. I don't know where to go. I'm scared Ashley. I don't know what to do. How did you keep him from waking up?"

Chris laughed when Ashley told her what Katie had done. The little girl was sleeping soundly in the backseat.

"Depends on how many she gave him. Problem may be over. He might not wake up at all. Where did she get the pills?" Ashley related what Katie had told her about hiding them from him. "Smart girl you have there. Reckon what she will think about seeing her real father for the first time?" Ashley seemed to shrink. Chris reached over and rubbed her sister's arm.

"It's okay, Ash. Everything will be ok."

"How did Kevin come to have all those letters? Where did Kevin come from? How does he know Brad?"

"I don't know the answers to those questions but we will find out soon enough. As soon as Brad and Daniel get back we will all talk this out and figure out what to do. I only read one of those letters and saw it was from Brad. I don't know what the rest of them say. Maybe there is more information in them."

They pulled up to Chris' house. Ashley hesitated before getting out.

"What if he does wake up and comes here to get me? I can't Chris. I can't be somewhere where he can find me. Please let me borrow your car. I want to get away from you and your family in case he comes looking. I don't want to cause you all any more trouble. This will be the first place he will look."

"You most certainly are not leaving my sight again. I have spent weeks worrying about you and not being able to get to you. We are in this together and we will stick together until the end. We will be okay." Chris gestured to her purse and Ashley looked down to see the handle of a pistol sticking out of it. She immediately looked back up at Chris in shock.

"Where did you get that?" she asked.

"Don't worry. You'll be fine, little sister," was all Chris said.

Katie

This was sort of scary. All of the adults were in the living room and all the kids were banished to Carley's bedroom. There was a strange man out there who kept looking at Katie funny whenever she went out of the bedroom. She didn't know him and now she was sort of scared of strangers. The last man she had trusted had been Kevin and he was scary now. She hoped that she hadn't really hurt Kevin by giving him those pills. She had only meant to make him sleep so she and Mom could get out of there.

Maybe that man was a police officer and he was going to take her to jail. She got up off the floor and went to sit in Carley's lap. Carley smelled good. She always had on good smelling lotion and lip gloss. Even this early in the morning she smelled good. Katie yawned. She had not slept much last night and now she was sleepy and she missed Rosie. Mommy hadn't thought about getting Rosie when they left last night. When she realized it, she had started to cry and beg Mom to go back and get her but Mom had shouted at her to be quiet. She didn't know what those adults could be discussing that was more important than getting Rosie away from Kevin. Slowly sleep overcame her and she rested.

Ashley

Tired lines formed around Ashley's eyes and she kept staring at Brad. Now that she knew what had happened she didn't have the burden of hate to carry around anymore. Seems like lately she was eating her words more and more. Who knew how much life could change in such a short period of time? She would have never guessed that she could forgive Brad for leaving Katie. Now she knew that sometimes things weren't as they seemed at first. Sometimes you had to look deeper to see the real meaning and sometimes love caused people to hurt the ones they loved most.

"Brad, I am really sorry for all you have been through." She let her eyes wander over his slight body and up to his dark eyes and auburn hair. He looked healthy at first glance but she knew him better than most. She had spent years loving him and she could see subtle details that indicated ill health. For instance, she noticed that there were more lines around his eyes. This could be just the years that had passed but she also saw the dark bruises like shadows under his eyes. His skin didn't seem as clear and vibrant either. He had lost a good bit of weight.

"Ashley, I don't even know how to imagine how hurt you must have been for all these years. I'll bet you hate me." This admission seemed to take most of his energy away and she saw him slouch further into the couch cushions. When he looked back up at her she saw something in his eyes that stunned her. He still loved her. She couldn't speak. All these years she had hated him and yet here he was loving her. Their worlds had been so different and yet the bottom line in this world was trying to make a difference. Maybe they had lost each other once, but she wouldn't let her anger and hate overcome whatever good she could do to help Brad.

"Brad, I'll be honest. I hated you with a passion so deep that it changed me. I never knew someone could take your heart out and stomp on it. That is what it felt like when you left me. I was so excited about having our baby and the whole time you had been planning your escape. I felt deceived and unlovable. I wondered what it was about me that you didn't like so much that you needed to leave. I wondered if I hadn't gotten pregnant if you would have stayed. Finally it hit me that my anger towards you was seeping through my pores and influencing my beautiful baby daughter. She didn't deserve to have a mother filled with hate and regret. So I poured myself into our Katie. I became a person that stopped to admire a pretty painting. I took time out of my day to play in the floor with her. I finally felt human again. I won't say that it was easy. But it was worth it all. She is the best part of me and I love her so much that my heart hurts."

Brad

He had been watching her face the whole time she was describing the last few years. She was beautiful. He had almost forgotten the strength of love. He had forgotten what love could cause you to do. Over the years he had convinced himself that it didn't matter anyway. Something would have happened to change the way she felt about him and eventually they would have split anyway. Now for the first time in years, he wondered. When he was with her he felt complete. He didn't feel sick and tired. Actually he felt better than he had in ages. Was that adrenaline running through his veins?

"Ashley, first I want to apologize. I realize now how stupid I was. When I found out that I was very sick I couldn't imagine putting you through all I was going to have to do. The doctor I went to in Atlanta told me that I only had, at the most, two years to live. Two years." He slowly shook his head from side to side and sighed.

"Not a very good prognosis for someone who is expecting to be a Dad very soon. I wondered if it would be better for everyone if I just left. Spare you and her the pain of watching me die. Better to just leave and maybe one day you would tell her good stories about me. In the end, that is exactly what I did. I moved to Los Angeles and started treatments right away. I was so sick I couldn't hold up my own head. All of my hair fell out and I was admitted to the hospital for numerous procedures. After a year the doctors saw some progress and I started to wonder if maybe I would make it after all. Then I had a full body scan and they discovered more cancer. This time it had metastasized to my liver and lungs. If I thought chemo was bad, then that was because I had yet to discover radiation. They hit me with all they could without killing me and I spent days wondering why they couldn't just go ahead and get it over with,"

"Finally the treatments were over and I could see daylight at the end of the tunnel. That is when I wrote the first letter. After being so close to death for so long I decided that I would apologize for leaving and beg you to forgive me. I waited for a month for you to respond one way or another. When you didn't I figured that you probably hated me for leaving you and wouldn't ever forgive me. I told myself that if I ever got completely better I was going to come back and beg you. I wanted to see my baby girl so badly. I never even got to see her. She is beautiful, Ashley. Just like I always expected her to be. Her hair is like mine!"

This made them both laugh. This had been a topic of discussion almost daily when they had found out they were expecting her. Both of them jumped at a sudden thump outside the door. Brad looked out the window and pronounced all was okay.

"Ashley, we can talk about all of this later. Right now you need to get help. Call the police and tell them what is going on. Kevin is going to come over here just as soon as he wakes up and when he does I don't want us to be unprepared."

"Brad, you keep talking about Kevin like you know him? Who is he? I need to know," she asked.

"Ashley, Kevin is my brother. His real name is Rick. Actually Richard Demore." She couldn't fathom this new information. What he was saying wasn't possible.

"Your brother? I have met all your brothers and I know that I never met him before. Please stop and tell me exactly what is going on. Don't mince words. Tell me all of it now, please." "About the time that I was getting finished with chemo a man came to the hospital to see me. He said that his name was Rick and that he was my brother. Of course I thought he was pulling my leg or had me mixed up with someone else but he insisted. Finally he brought me a picture of my mother. That got my attention. He said that my mother had been married to his father and they had had him. His father died and Mom left him to live with his aunt. He never saw her again. I didn't believe any of this. You know how my mother was. She loved everybody."

"Loved? Are you saying that in the past tense?" she asked.

"Yes. I am afraid that I lost my mom two years ago." Ashley felt sorry for him because she knew how close they had been.

"I am so sorry, Brad. I didn't know."

"It's ok. She got really sick. Anyway, I went to my mom and flat out asked her about Rick. You should have seen her face, Ashley. I had never seen her look that way before." His voice trailed off at the memory.

"She told me to stay away from him. She said that if he was anything like his father then he was no good. Then she turned her back on me and walked away. Walked away. Can you picture this from my mother?"

"Absolutely not, Brad. There was obviously a lot more to that that she couldn't speak of. What happened next?"

"Well, Rick kept coming to visit with me. He brought food and magazines and things to help pass the time. He was there when I vomited twenty six times in one night. He held my hand when I wanted to die. I told him all about you. I thought that I wouldn't make it so I told him everything. I just wanted someone else on this earth to remember me. When I would write these letters to you he would take them to mail them. Evidently he never did. You see, Chris found all of my letters bound up with string. They were in your babysitter's house, Ashley. She must have found them and didn't know what to do. Before she could do anything Rick killed her. I know that you didn't do it. He has killed before and he will do it again if we don't stop him."

"I don't understand. Why would he have taken your letters? Why did he come here?"

"Well think about it, honey. He knew all about you and I described you as you are. Beautiful, loving, kind, hard working. I even told him about your dream to fix up that old house on Holder Lane. I told him about your love of onion rings and hot dogs. I told him about your favorite color. He took everything I told him and put it in memory and came out here to sweep you off your feet."

191

Brad realized that Ashley was no longer listening to him. He leaned forward and softly touched her shoulder to get her to face him. When she spun around suddenly he instinctively ducked. The anger and hurt on her face broke his heart all over again. What had he done to the woman of his dreams?

Ashley

"I don't believe it! There is no way that he listened to you talk and remembered all of this with the intention of coming here. That is ludicrous. All of this has just been a farce? He doesn't love me at all. He tricked me. I loved him, Brad. I trusted him with my daughter and I fell for it all hook, line and sinker. I must be the most stupid woman on earth. Surely I should have seen through all of this."

He winced when she slammed her palm into her forehead.

"No, Ashley. Rick is a very sick, yet very intelligent person. I'm sorry to say this but he has done this before. Before he came to meet me he had been in prison for fifteen years for murder. He told me about it, but he said that he was changed and I believed it. I fell for him too. I think he truly believes that he loves you. That is why he is so dangerous. He fell in love with you from my storytelling. He believes that this is his real life and you are in love with him and he will do whatever is necessary to protect his dream."

"Brad, you don't realize how far he took this. He did come here and sweep me off of my feet. We live in that house on Holder Lane." She stopped while Brad stared at her in disbelief. This realization made both of them quiet for a moment.

"Brad, how am I ever going to get this straightened out? What am I supposed to do? How can I stop him? I'm not crazy you know. He told everybody that I was, but really he has been drugging me. I see it now. He even told me that Chris had come on to him. It worked just like he planned. I got so mad at her that I haven't talked to her in a long time."

"It's all okay. We are going to get this figured out. Let's go get some food and talk this out with your family. But please be prepared for all of this to get worse before it gets better."

Chris

She kept looking towards the door and expecting to see Kevin—Rick. Whoever he was. She kept thinking about that night when he had come here before and remembering the look in his eyes. She should have known then and she didn't understand why she hadn't pursued it more. No, she had let Ashley talk her into believing that everything was okay. Living in dreamland gets us nowhere, she thought. Time to face the facts. The fact was that Kevin was a sick man. He was extremely dangerous because he truly believed his own lies. She reached to the small of her back and felt the handle of the pistol and instantly felt a little bit better. "He might come here, but I'll be damned if he will take Ashley or Katie away. I will kill him first."

Carley

She woke to the sound of pots and pans being banged around. She smelled bacon and her mouth instantly began to water. Had they eaten dinner last night? She couldn't remember. Everything had gotten crazy. She couldn't believe that Brad was back. Now that she was seeing him she remembered more about him. He had taught her how to blow a bubble with gum. They had laughed and laughed when she finally got it right and the gum popped all over her face. How had she forgotten? He had always been so nice and she wondered why he had left. Oh well, not to worry. Surely someone would tell her the whole story soon enough. She turned over in bed and felt for Katie. That sweet girl had slept like a rock.

She knew it must be late morning because of the way the sunlight was coming into her window. So they had missed school? This must be a big deal if Mom and Dad had allowed that to happen. They never even let her stay out of school when she was sick unless she was running a fever of 106 or foaming at the mouth.

"Katie, wake up." No response. "Katie?" Carley sat up and looked around. Maybe she was already up and in the kitchen. She lay back down and ran her hands over her hair. Need to get up and shower before she went in for breakfast. She must look a mess.

Daniel

Secretly, he was worried about Kevin coming here. He couldn't believe that he had spent time talking and drinking with him. What if that psycho tried to tear down the door to get to Ashley? Sure, he and Brad were here but there were entirely too many people here for them to try to protect. Sort of made him regret not owning a gun. He never thought he would say that. What kind of help would Brad be? He was weak and skinny and this was his brother, for goodness sakes. Chris was calling everybody to eat breakfast. He guessed that he needed to round up the kids since he didn't hear the sound of footsteps bounding into the kitchen. Everybody was tired this morning, but he knew how much it irritated her when people didn't come eat when she had cooked. Goodness knows that she didn't need any more stress.

Suddenly he heard a piercing scream. Ashley was screaming for Katie. Where in the world was she? He had checked on her and Carley just a while ago. Probably just in the bathroom. He couldn't blame Ashley for being worried. She was bound to be overwrought. Poor Ashley, she didn't deserve this. She was one of the best people he knew and it made him furious that Kevin had lied to all of them. He jumped when Ashley screamed again. She sounded more alarmed now. She was running down the hallway shouting that Katie was gone. Oh Lord, where was that little girl?

Ashley

Katie was not in the house. At all. She had disappeared and Ashley didn't know where to start looking for her. Chris was trying to calm her down but Ashley could see that Chris was just as scared as she was. They were both trembling and Ashley was trying her best to not panic. She needed to think. Everybody was gathered in the kitchen looking at her for direction. She gazed around at all of their concerned faces and tried to decide what to do first. She reached for the phone and did what she should have done last night. She dialed 911.

After giving a brief description of Katie to the dispatcher she handed the phone to Chris. She didn't feel like she could waste her time when Katie was out there somewhere alone. Had Kevin gotten into the house and taken her?

"Daniel, Brad, Carley, Drew? Did any of you see Katie this morning? When was the last time you saw her?"

"I checked on her about an hour ago, Ashley. She was sleeping peacefully in Carley's bed."

So he couldn't have came and taken her because they would have seen or heard him. The only other option was that Katie had slipped out the back door and left.

"Why would she have left? Anybody know of any reason that Katie would feel like she should leave here?" As soon as the words left her mouth she knew without a doubt where Katie was headed.

"Rosie! Oh my God, she is going back to his house to get her dog, Rosie. An hour. How far could a five year old go in an hour? Could she find the house on her own?" Now she was going to panic. A five year old walking two miles without guidance or protection with Kevin out there angry. Chris finished on the phone.

"Police will be here in a minute. What? Ashley what is up?" She could see that Ashley was about to lose it. Daniel stepped over to Ashley and put his arms around her.

"Ashley, we will split up and find her in no time. If not, then someone we know will surely see her walking on the road and pick her up and bring her home." He must have realized his mistake as soon as he said it because he let her go and went for his keys.

"I'm going to Kevin's house right now. You guys branch out and start looking. Call my cell phone if you find her before I do. Chris, you wait here for the police. Tell them that Katie may be at Kevin's and to come there immediately."

Ashley seemed to find relief in him taking control. She ran out to his car and got in the passenger seat. When he got in and tried to argue with her she held up her hand.

"Daniel, this is my daughter we are talking about. I am not going to discuss this with you."

"Yes, ma'am." And he started the car and threw gravel in the yard in his haste to leave.

Kevin

Damn he was confused. Why had he slept so hard and where in the hell was Ashley? He needed to be packing and getting ready to leave and he couldn't find her. Maybe she had gone outside to that shed of hers. No that couldn't be right because Katie would be with her and wherever Katie went so did that mutt of hers. Rosie was sitting by the front door whining. He tried throwing a shoe at her and missed. She gave him a look that seemed to tell him she hated him. He laughed out loud. "See how you like it around here later on today, little bitch. Gonna be a little bit lonely."

Just as soon as he found Ashley and Katie he would pack up and move on. He knew that Ashley would be happy to be rid of that sister of hers. It had to be stifling to be needed like that. That woman was too nosy for her own good. He would have to be careful or she would track them down. He felt it in his bones. Have to be very careful. That's ok. I've dealt with her kind before. Ask them how he handled it. At this he laughed again. Hard to ask them because they were dead! Took care of them once and for all. Tired to death of nosy people. Just him and Ashley and Katie. All living together with no one to bother them. That's just what he needed.

He heard a sound in the kitchen and Rosie took off like a shot in that direction. Oh good. They must be back.

"Rosie! Good girl! Come on, we need to hurry and get away from here. Kevin is mean and Mommy is getting us away from here. We've got to get back to Chris and the police are going to come get Kevin. I am so sorry we left you behind."

"Well, well, little Katie. Glad to see that you know where your loyalties lie. Good choice to come back for your little puppy. "He noticed how scared she looked when she saw him standing in the doorway. Sort of made him wonder why she would be scared of him. Probably that stupid aunt of hers putting ideas in her head.

"Don't be scared of me, Katie. I would never hurt you, precious girl. Come see me." He held out his hands and took a step towards her. She backed up a step to match his. Puzzled, he stopped. "Where is your mommy honey? I need her. Can you tell me why she left?"

Ashley

She knew that Katie had made it to the house. She was a smart little girl and she was determined. How could she have thought that Katie would just not worry about her dog? She loved her with all her heart and would have felt lost without her. The only question was if Kevin was awake and how she would get Katie away if he was.

Daniel slowed down as they approached Kevin's house. Nothing seemed out of the ordinary on the outside. Who know what turmoil was going on inside? When the car stopped, she jumped out and ran up the steps of the porch. She opened the door and peered inside. No one was in the living room. She crept into the house and slowly looked around. Everything seemed the same as when she had left. She jumped a mile when Daniel came up behind her and touched her on the shoulder.

"Daniel!" she whispered in agitation.

"Sorry. I could hardly let you go in here alone," he whispered back.

They both jumped at the sound of a crash upstairs. Without thinking, Ashley started running through the house and shouting Katie's name. Another crash rapidly followed the first one. She raced up the stairs two at a time and almost collided with Kevin at the top. He was holding two suitcases in one hand and Katie's hand with the other one. Katie looked scared and Rosie was shaking by her side.

"Ashley, good you're home. Just in time to help me pack. Got to get out of here. Time to move on, honey." He pushed her to the side and continued on down the stairs. Just then he noticed Daniel in hot pursuit coming up the stairs.

"What is he doing here?"

"Kevin, please. Let's go downstairs and talk. We need to discuss something." He stared hard at Daniel and then Ashley. He seemed to be putting things together in his head.

201

"What's going on around here? Katie said something about the police. Ashley, why are the police coming? I haven't done anything wrong. I love you, sweetheart. I tried to cover for you, honey. I knew that they would be coming to take Katie from you and I just made you seem fragile. No harm done."

Ashley stared at him like she had never seen him before. Kevin hated it when people looked at him like that. Like they didn't know what they expected him to do next. Sometimes in prison the other inmates had looked at him like that and he felt isolated and scared. He wanted to be a part of things, not alone. He had made quite a name for himself in the joint. Spent most of his stay in isolation because people wouldn't stop watching him. Now his own wife was acting like he was crazy. Before he could stop himself he punched her in the eyes. Now she couldn't stare at him like that.

Brad

Darn it she had left him here to look around. Like Katie would be anywhere near here. If she was going to get her dog she would be there by now. A five year old could cover a lot of ground in one hour. The sound of sirens interrupted his thoughts. Good, they were here. Maybe someone would go help Ashley and Daniel. He walked up the driveway just as the police cruiser arrived. Chris ran out to tell them about what was going on. The officer had a hard time following all the ins and outs of the unusual situation but Brad could see that he was concerned. A little girl missing and a crazy man. Small town cops nightmare. Brad wondered if the guy had ever been involved with a case like this before. More than likely not. Around here a case of petty theft or vandalism were probably the hot cases. Brad walked up and introduced himself.

"The man we are worried about is my brother. He is using an alias. His name is really Richard Demure. He has a prison record and a history of mental problems. The little girl who is missing is my daughter, Katie. Please help us, officer."

Daniel

Kevin launched himself at Daniel with a seemingly inhuman force. He pinned Daniel to the wall beside the door and began punching him in the stomach with his fist. Daniel slouched over to try to protect himself. He had trouble breathing and the punches kept coming. He shoved hard with his hands and pushed off the wall with one leg. This caused Kevin to be thrown off balance and he went down hard onto his back. From a few feet away Daniel heard Katie crying. This gave him the strength he needed to jump on top of Kevin and punch him as hard as he could in the face. Kevin fought him off and rolled over. Like a cat he seemed to leap up and land on his feet. Daniel had never seen anyone pull off a move like that one, except in movies. Before he had time to register that Kevin was back on his feet he had been forced into the wall. One hard blow landed on the side of his head and blackness closed in.

Chris

Chris had never in her life felt such rage. She felt like she immediately became a different person and this new person had no fear. She only knew that she was not going to let this bastard hurt her sister like that ever again. She hardly recognized herself. It felt like time slowed to a crawl and she was moving as if underwater. She ran to her car and started the engine. She barely registered Brad jumping into the passenger side. She drove directly to Kevin's house and jumped out of the car. She reached back with her right hand and removed the pistol from her waistband.

Brad inhaled sharply but she didn't hear him. She raced into the house without a second thought. Standing right there in front of her was her worst fear. Lying at his feet was her husband, Daniel and her sister, Ashley. Katie was nowhere to be seen. When she pointed it at Kevin she knew in that second that she was going to kill him. That is what it would take to stop him.

"Kevin. Rick. Whoever in the hell you are. Stop right there." He looked up as if surprised to see her there. Blood was gushing from Ashley's head.

"Well if it's not the protective sister again. What do you think you are going to do with that pistol? Be careful or you might hurt someone. Do you even know what to do with it? It's not even loaded." He laughed without an ounce of fear. This made Chris a little bit unsure of herself but she kept the barrel pointed at him.

"If you move another step we will both find out. I need you to stay right there where you are until the police get here. If you don't do as I say, I will kill you right here and now."

Brad

Brad didn't think his hair could stick up that far. He had never encountered a moment in his life where he was so sure of what someone was saying. There was no hint of retreat or fear in Chris' voice. He waited for the pistol to fire at Rick. He was certain that Chris was going to shoot him right then. He saw her finger tense up on the trigger and Rick must have too, for he held up his hands and took a step back.

"Chris, don't do anything stupid. Katie is right around the corner and the last thing she needs is to see someone else getting shot."

Brad wondered at Rick's uncanny ability to say exactly the right thing at the right time. Chris glanced towards the kitchen and Rick lunged at her. Brad saw Chris' arm bend at an impossible angle when Rick's body came down on her in an effort to dislodge the gun. Just as they both went down Brad heard the crack of the gun and then his vision narrowed down to a pinpoint. A strange heaviness began in his chest but he didn't feel any pain. Blackness overcame him.

Katie

Katie loved to hide under her bed whenever she was scared. Used to Mom would tell her that monsters were not real but Katie knew that even Mom knew better than that now. Monsters were real. She reached out her arm to embrace Rosie. It was amazing how much Rosie had grown. Her fur was long and soft and had gotten lighter in color in the past few weeks. Whenever she lay down next to Rosie she was just as long as her. Katie heard some loud noises downstairs but she didn't dare go to investigate. Mom was probably very mad at her for coming back here.

"It's okay, Rosie. It was worth it to get to you." Rosie licked her on the nose and Katie almost smiled. Then she heard another sound coming from the living room. She heard heavy footsteps on the stairs and peeked out from under the covers to see who was here. She recognized Kevin's boots coming into her room.

"Katie! Come out here right now!" Sounded like he meant business. She crawled out from under the bed and stood up. Without waiting for her to follow he turned and started throwing clothes into a suitcase.

"Where are we going?" she asked in alarm. She knew that he would never let her take Rosie with them on a trip because he was mad at her for chewing up things.

"Stop asking questions. You will see when we get there."

A few minutes later Katie found herself in the car with Kevin and Mommy and Rosie. Kevin was so mad that she could see a vein bulging in his head. She had thought that only in cartoons did people do that, but now she could see it was true. Seemed like everything that was supposed to be pretend was true. She would have to think about that later on. For now she had to make sure that Rosie was a good dog and minded Kevin. He hadn't wanted to take her with them but he had been in such a hurry that he didn't have time for Katie's tantrum. She smiled.

Mommy was awake now and sitting up in the front seat. She was holding her eyes and Katie could see that she had a dark bruise across the top of her nose. Honestly, Katie was a little bit mad at Mom. If she had of thought of Rosie in the first place then Katie wouldn't have had to go back for her. It had been a long night and then a long walk home and Katie found that she was tired. She curled up in the back seat next to her precious doggie and went to sleep.

Ashley

Darn it, her head hurt. She needed an ice pack. She needed an aspirin. What she really needed was to be able to go back in time and think about what she was doing before she married Kevin. What in the world had possessed her to marry a man she hardly knew? Well, she was getting to know the real man now. She didn't even know him by his real name. She would have to try to use Rick. Rick Demore. An ex-con and murderer and who knew what else. And she had allowed herself to be manipulated and lied to. She had put her life and her daughter's like in jeopardy for the sake of love. Love. What a joke. The only love she knew was her love for Katie.

She looked back over her shoulder to check on Katie, sound asleep curled up with Rosie. Stupid dog. She smiled to herself. No one would ever say that Katie didn't take care of the ones she loved. She might have gotten them in big trouble, but by golly she had her dog.

"Where are we going?" she asked Rick. He took his time in answering and gripped the steering wheel tighter. He was clinching his teeth too and Ashley knew that he only did this when he was nervous. Maybe she could use this knowledge to her advantage. "If you are scared of getting in trouble with the police you could just let us out right now and disappear. No one will know where you are headed. I won't even try to find you."

"Yeah right, Ashley. I am so sure that you are willing to just start right back over where you were before you met me. You don't want justice or money, right? You will just get you a little job and a little house and you and Katie will continue on with your little lives. You need me, Ashley. You need me to be someone."

Was he serious? Did he really think that she couldn't live without him? She had been making it just fine for all those years before she met him. Of course, Rick wasn't rational and he wasn't thinking clearly. Where in the world was he taking them? She needed to figure out a way to get away from him before they got too far from home. Around here she knew her way and all the people. Much farther on and she would be alone. To her surprise the car lurched to a stop and Rick looked around her to the side of the road. He seemed to be searching for something. She peered into the woods to see whatever had caused him to stop. "It's right around here somewhere. Right here."

He made a quick U-turn and drove the car down a dirt road that was nearly hidden by overgrown grass and branches. She vaguely remembered this road from somewhere before. He didn't even slow down when the road became almost too rough to drive on. The underside of the car scraped on sharp rocks and Katie sat up in the backseat.

"Mommy, I need to use the bathroom," she said sleepily. "Hey, where are we? Are we going camping?" she asked in wonder. That is when Ashley realized where he was headed. Back when she and Brad had first met he had taken her to his hunting cabin in the woods. They had stayed there overnight a time or two and gone fishing in the river and grilled the trout they caught. She had almost forgotten all about it. Now she remembered how secluded the cabin had been. Not many people even knew it existed at all. Ashley wondered when the last time someone had ventured down this old road.

"Why are we going here? What are we going to do? Rick? We don't even have food or water. Please say something." "I see that you remember this place after all, huh? Old love shack from the past. I got a lot of info from my old brother when he thought he was going to die. Down to the last detail of how to get here. Of course, I never knew I would need to come here. Just kept that information up my sleeve in case of an emergency. This is what I would consider an emergency. The police are bound to be looking for your car. I remembered just exactly where to go. No one should ever say that I am stupid." He laughed loudly.

Ashley didn't know how to reach him. He was obviously completely off his rocker. He had just shot and probably killed his brother and still had yet to show an ounce of remorse. "Rick, did you kill Brad? Do you think he is dead?" Rick looked over at her with such surprise that she wondered if she had dreamed up the whole thing.

"Kill Brad? Now why would I do that? I love him. I am sure that he is just fine and dandy. We are brothers by blood. Of course, that stupid mother of ours was a whore. Did you know that she left me? Yes, she did. She up and left me with my aunt and never looked back. Brad didn't even know I existed at all until I came to the hospital to see him. She deserved to die a slow death and I made sure that she did. Poor Brad, it was hard to watch him suffer because he just couldn't see how she really was."

Ashley was horrified. For the first time, she realized that he was seriously going to kill her and Katie if she didn't do something. She wondered if he realized what he was doing. "What are we going to do out here, Rick? As far as I know there was only one cabin and it was old and broken down years ago. There are no supplies or fresh water."

"Don't worry, honey. Kevin will take care of you like he always does. Haven't I made you happy? That stupid Rick is nothing but trouble. He will kill you and Katie if I let him. Don't worry. I love you and Katie and I will protect you from him." He looked in the rearview mirror and then glanced from side to side. "You don't see him anywhere do you? I think we lost him."

Chris

Things had gotten so out of hand now. She remembered pointing the pistol at Kevin and then he jumped on top of her and the gun went off. She distinctly remembered feeling shocked that it had actually fired. Then he had hit her so hard that she must have been knocked unconscious. Now she felt helpless and puzzled. Brad was lying on his back and there was so much blood around him that she just knew that he was dead. She had killed him? Oh, God help me, she thought. She moaned and tried to sit up. Daniel was starting to regain consciousness, too. He rolled over and tried to focus on the scene around him.

"Chris? Are you ok? What happened?" Chris lost all hope of trying to remain calm. Daniel's eyes were swollen and blood covered most of his face. She figured that she must look much the same. Tears started and wouldn't stop. Where were the stupid cops?

"We need to get help for Brad, Daniel. I think the gun went off when Kevin landed on me and he was shot." She wasn't sure how Daniel understood what she had said at all because her words were muffled by her swollen lip and she was weeping so hard. She saw Daniel get up and go to Brad's side as if scared to look at him. Gently, he felt for a pulse in his neck.

"He's alive, barely. We need help now." Daniel took off for the telephone and called 911. She listened with half an ear to him telling the dispatcher where they were. She wondered where he had taken Ashley and Katie. She didn't know how long she had been out, but it seemed like a while. The blood around Brad had congealed so it must at least have been a few minutes. How far could he have gotten in such a short time?

Kevin

Things were not going so well at all. He hadn't been quite ready to move on yet. He still had a few more preparations to make before they took off to Montana. Now things had been forced on him and he didn't like being forced to do anything. Being in prison for fifteen years made a man tired of being told what to do. On the day he had been released he had promised himself to be in charge of his life from now on. No more orders, no more demands. Everything had been so good for a while there. Then Rick had shown up and things had gotten a little tricky.

Rick was crazy. He resorted to violence when he didn't get his way and Kevin knew that violence wasn't the answer. Brains were the answer. He had learned to sit back and plan every move he made and then things went according to plan. Rick had been the one to get him in prison in the first place. After years of therapy in prison, Rick had moved on and Kevin hadn't seen him for years until a few weeks ago. Kevin opened the door to the cabin and pushed Ashley and Katie inside in front of him. Cobwebs glistened in the air and the spiders scurried to get away from these intruders. It was evident that no one had been in here for a while. Dust was thick on all surfaces of the furniture and the place had a musty smell. He moved to open the windows to let in fresh air.

"We can't stay here, Kevin." Ashley was persistent when she wanted to be.

"Ashley, I will decide where we will stay. We have to stay away from the roads until the cops stop looking for us. Don't you realize, honey, that we have to get away from here and we have to be smart about it." He shook his head in wonder. Sometimes that woman could be so dumb. She acted like she didn't have a brain in her head. Of course he wasn't stupid enough to come here without supplies. Planning. It was all in the plans and he had been planning this for months.

He went back outside and breathed in a deep breath of fresh air. Looking around him in wonder, he decided that a man could have picked a less desirable place to stay for a few weeks. This place was beautiful and it was a shame that no one used it. He could hear the sound of the river from a distance. Later on maybe he could take his little girl fishing. Surely there were fishing poles around here somewhere and he knew that Katie would treasure the time with him. He opened the trunk of the car and lifted the box of food from it. Just staples, but it would get them through a few weeks. Rice and beans and flour and water. A few cans of meat and some sugar. Even had canned and powdered milk. Living like the pioneers, he thought with a smile. He could turn this into an adventure. Ashley would love it!

"Hey, Ashley, can you come help me carry in all these gallons of water?" He loved seeing the look of surprise on her face. Goodness, he loved this woman! When she looked at him like that, his heart almost exploded with love.

Carley

Mom had raced out of here without even thinking about her and Drew. Oh well, who cared about them with all this excitement going on? The police officers were outside and inside scouring the place for any trace of Katie. Carley was worried about her. She knew that Kevin was a madman and Katie was in serious danger if she had gone back over there. How long had it taken her to walk over to Ashley's the other day? She thought about it and decided that maybe forty minutes would be a good guess. She hadn't been in any hurry and she had kept dodging cars so no one would see her. If Katie had been running she could easily have been back home in thirty five minutes. Now she had been gone for three hours. She heard the crackle of the police radio and turned to listen to the dispatcher. All of the officers heard the plea for help from out at Ashley's house and took off running towards their cruisers. Carley had heard the dispatcher say that a man had been shot in the chest and was near death. Paramedics had been dispatched to the scene and a man, woman and child were missing and they believed the woman and child had been taken against their will. The lady said to be on the lookout for a car matching Ashley sedan's description. Carley sank down on the steps of the front porch and started to cry. She just knew that either her dad or Brad had been shot and was dead. There had been no mention of her mom and she didn't know what to do. Slowly she got up and took Drew by the hand and led him back inside the house to stay until someone told her what was going on.

Katie

This place was neat. Her mom had told her that they would be staying here for a while until she figured out a way to get home. In one room there were bunk beds and a little tiny bathroom with only enough room for a potty and a shower. The kitchen looked like a doll house kitchen with little cabinets and a little sink. Everything was dirty, though and Mom had been cleaning for forever. Kevin was walking around whistling and smiling and for a few minutes everything was back to the way it used to be. Kevin had told her a while ago that later on he was going to take her fishing. She was so excited but still a little bit scared of him. She never knew when she would do something to make him mad and he would be mean again.

She grabbed her jacket and ran out the door with Rosie close at her heels. She had seen a log earlier that she wanted to investigate. This thing was huge! She could see all the way through it in the middle. If she tried really hard she wondered if she would fit inside of it. Maybe not today for there were spiders and ants crawling all over it. Rosie sniffed at some plants and barked. She pounced on an ant and pretended to stalk a butterfly. Katie climbed up on the log and sat down to survey her surroundings. She could see Kevin in front of the house chopping wood. He seemed so happy that she almost didn't recognize him. She looked closely for any sign of the mean Kevin, but he acted normal. He was whistling.

Ashley

She could only imagine the worry her family was feeling. Little did they know that Ashley was only a few miles away playing "camp" with Kevin and Katie. She knew that Chris must be beside herself with concern. If she were still alive.

Shut up! She mentally chided herself. There was no way she could do what needed to be done if she started thinking things like that. She had to be strong and sure and smart. She had to bide her time until the time came when she saw a way out. She lifted her hair from her neck and fanned herself with her other hand. She had beads of sweat on her brow and she knew that she needed to shower. With a glance, she dismissed the bathroom. She was entirely too tired to tackle that shower tonight. Darkness was falling and she needed to get something started for dinner. Katie had to be tired after all of the playing she had done today. Ashley had to admit that Katie was enjoying herself. She and Rosie had played all day around the cabin.

She decided to make some biscuits and grits. Katie loved grits. Ashley wondered what she was supposed to feed Rosie. As much as Kevin hated her lately, she knew that he hadn't brought dog food. She would just have to eat the scraps left over from their dinner. This decided, she began mixing the flour and Crisco. How long would Kevin be happy? How long before Rick decided to rear his ugly head and she and Katie were in danger?

She wondered if she needed to go ahead and take a chance and try to slip away tonight. She looked outside at Kevin chopping wood with an axe he had produced from the trunk. Had he thought of everything? No wonder he had spent so much time out in that shed of his. He evidently had a stash of emergency escape supplies ready to go at a moment's notice. She wondered if he had a gun. She wished she still had hers. Where would he take them after leaving here? Did he already have a special place picked out for them to spend the rest of their happy lives? She was angry and she was sick and tired of being bullied by him. She threw the biscuit dough harder than necessary down on the counter. First chance she got, she and Katie were out of here!

Chris

It had been more than a week since Ashley and Katie had disappeared with him. She hadn't slept or eaten much of anything since then. She had to find them. Where could they have gone so quickly? The police had set up road blocks all over the county and none of them had produced a single lead. Seemed like they had dropped off the face of the earth. Of course, he could have changed cars, but surely Ashley's abandoned car would have been found by now, right?

Daniel was so worried about her. He had taken to watching her whenever he didn't know she was paying attention to him. She knew that there had to be a way to find them but she couldn't figure it out yet. Carley was more and more rebellious and hurtful. She had screamed at Chris yesterday that she was a bad mother. Maybe she was.

She decided to go to the hospital to visit with Brad again today. As soon as he regained consciousness she wanted to ask him some questions. The doctors were shocked that he was still alive. The bullet had ripped through his chest cavity and torn muscles and his heart had stopped. They were keeping him sedated now so that his body could heal.

She walked down the pristine corridor and noticed the antiseptic smell that medical facilities seemed to radiate. She smelled the sweet smell of roses that drifted from a patient's room down the hallway. She peeked into the partly open doorway of Brad's room. To her surprise he was sitting up in bed. His eyes were closed and he had next to no color on his face. She ventured a few steps inside the room and tentatively cleared her throat. Immediately he opened his eyes and blinked several times as if to clear his vision.

"Chris?" She let out her held breath and relaxed measurably.

"Brad, I am so glad to see you awake. You have been out for a while." She went to him and took his hand in hers. His fingers felt cold and lifeless. His grip was weak.

"You look like shit. Sorry to say that, but you do. I hate to even ask, but I have to know. Are they dead? Did he kill them?" He looked deeply into her eyes as if searching for the answer. Chris felt a single tear roll down her cheek as she shook her head.

"Brad, he just put them in the car and vanished. I don't know if my sister is alive or dead. No one has any clue as to where they are."

She started to cry in earnest now. Brad tried to comfort her as best as he could. Relief poured over him. There was still hope. If he hadn't killed them right then, there was still hope of finding them before he did. He had to get better and get out of here. He tried to rise up off the pillow behind his head, but found that he couldn't move more than an inch. Piercing pain took his breath away and he felt lightheaded. Chris noticed what he was trying to do and pressed him back into the bed.

"Brad, you have been very, very sick. You can't get up at all yet. Please forgive me for breaking down like that."

She wiped her eyes with the back of her hand and then straightened his sheets. "Chris? Listen to me carefully. I am going to help you find them. I can't talk any more right now, but I am going to find them. I promise you that I will. I have waited for so long to be with them and I won't let him take them away from me."

This exhausted all of his energy and within seconds he was asleep. Chris stayed only a few more minute and then quietly slipped out of his room. She needed to go to work but she just couldn't get back into doing normal stuff, not with her sister out there somewhere needing her help.

Kevin

He felt the point of the stick he had been whittling and smiled in wonder. He couldn't believe he still remembered how to do this Boy Scout stuff. He should win some kind of award for all the stuff he had done this week. He laughed out loud at this. His Scouts leader had kicked him out of their club when he was seven because he had killed a couple of animals at the yearly overnight camping adventure. Those boys had cried and ran for the scout leader. Little sissies, all of them. What was the big deal about dead squirrels, anyway? Decapitating them had been fun!

Who needed to know how to build a fire with twigs? If you planned ahead, you would have gasoline and matches! Humph! Who needed all those goodie goodies telling him what to do? He had made it just fine without them, although he had taken great pleasure in doing things that made them scream.

His aunt had slapped him around when she found out what he had done and then smoked another joint with her new boyfriend. She always had some man around. Mostly they left him alone, but this one seemed different.

"No good, that's what he is. No wonder his mama left him here with me. He won't ever be any good for anything. Stupid, bratty little psycho."

The new boyfriend had laughed and stared at him.

"He is a cute little thing, though you know it?" And then they both had stared at him and laughed at him. Kevin wanted to slap that smile off of their faces.

That night he had been ready when he had came into his room. The flash of steel in the moonlight was picture perfect. The blade had lodged in his neck and he never even made a sound.

Ashley

Ashley was tired of waiting. She sort of wished that he would decide to do something so that the suspense would be over. Surely he didn't plan on them staying here forever. Someone could come down here looking around at any time and his cover would be blown. She found herself listening with half an ear for the sound of a vehicle. It was wearing her out, being on guard all the time.

Granted, Kevin had been as good as gold this past week. He had been pleasant and caring to both her and Katie. He had even taken a liking to Rosie and petted her more often now. If he thought that she had forgotten about how crazy he was, then he was wrong. She might play the docile little wife but she wasn't going to be carted off to another state and live in solitude for the rest of her life.

Last night she had decided to do an experiment. After she was sure that he was deeply asleep she had risen from the bed on the floor and tiptoed out the front door. Since there was no bedroom they were all sleeping in the front room with her and Katie on a blanket on the floor and him on the ragged sofa. She waited for a second to see if he would awaken and stop her but all she heard was his snoring. Taking this as a good sign, she continued on down the overgrown path to the river. This little experiment had proven to her that she could sneak off from him. Now, could she do the same thing with Katie and still get by with it? Would Rosie bark and give them away? Would Katie cry out in alarm and wake him up?

Lost in contemplation, she sat down on Katie's log to think. When Kevin spoke from not more than six inches from her back she jumped a foot and swung around to stare at him in surprise.

"Have a nice little walk?" he asked. Her heart was thumping and her hands trembled.

"Kevin? What are you doing up? I hope I didn't awaken you. I just felt like getting some fresh air." She could see by the moonlight that his eyes were angry. She moved a little closer to him and held out her hands.

"Let's go back inside and go to sleep."

He slapped her hands away and took her roughly in his arms. "You are mine, you understand? We belong together and no one is going to change that. Anybody who even tries will be dead before they even know I am there."

She could smell his sweat and hear him breathing in her ear. He was breathing hard and rubbing her back roughly with his hands. She was afraid of him. Like a wild animal sensing fear in its prey, he grabbed her even closer and kissed her with such violence that she panicked and tried to back away. He was revolting to her in every sense. She wiped her mouth with the back of her hand and nearly gagged. Kevin seemed hurt at her for rebuking his advances. He let her go without a fight, much to her surprise, causing her to stumble on a root in her hurry to get away from him.

"Go on, Ashley. You can run away but you will never leave me. We belong together. No matter where you go, I will find you. Go ahead and try. You won't get far." She still heard him laughing when she pushed through the cabin door. She fell on her knees beside of Katie and took her in her arms. Katie rustled sleepily in her arms. She held her there in her arms and rocked her gently. She had to figure out a way to get her out of here. Her precious baby didn't deserve to be living like this.

After a while she heard the door creak open and she sensed Kevin's return. She didn't even look up at him. She had already seen more of him than she needed to see.

Brad

He felt a little more energy returning every day and today he felt like he could walk. The two nurses held him up on each side to be sure he wouldn't fall. This was a scene he had played before. Many times in the past few years people had had to help him walk when the treatments had been almost too much for him. Goodness, he must have nine lives, like a cat. Two bouts with cancer and now he had been shot in the chest and lived to tell about it. Maybe after all of this was over he might write a book, he thought with a laugh. He might do something dangerous like sky diving or cave exploring. The doctor had told him that if the bullet had been just one-forth of an inch to the right, he would be a goner.

He made it to the end of the corridor and back without tiring too badly. Yes, he was winded but he hadn't fallen down either. One tough little cookie. He had just been tucked back into bed when Chris knocked softly on the door. He wasn't surprised to see her. She had stopped by every day since he had been here to check on him and to bring him some sort of cake or something she had made. Today she brought him the local newspaper and tossed it on the bed.

"What's up in the big town of Clarkston today?" he joked with her. When she didn't answer he looked into her eyes and saw fear reflected there. "What? What has happened?"

"They have called off the search for Ashley and Katie. The police have absolutely no leads. Brad, they are not going to look for them anymore."

With this she broke down and wept. Brad felt so helpless. Where could Rick have taken them? He had only lived here a short while and surely didn't know any place to hide out. Where would Brad go if he needed to evade the police? Suddenly Brad felt a surge of hope. Had he ever mentioned that place to Rick? He honestly couldn't remember what all he had talked about with him.

"Chris, I need to get out of here. I just thought of a place where no one has probably looked. It is a long shot, but I really need to go check there."

Chris looked at him skeptically. She raised an eyebrow at his feeble attempt to get out of bed.

"And you are going to go charging out there and save the day? Find Ashley and Katie and rescue them from your mad brother? The police have searched every spot within twenty miles of here. What kind of superhero are you?"

Brad had to smile at Chris with her hands on her hips and disbelief on her face. This is the Chris he knew. Full of life and spirit. She had been so down since all of this happened.

"I know it seems crazy, but I have to go look at a place that only a few people know about. It is an old fishing and hunting cabin deep in the woods. I may have told Rick about it. If we go by what he has remembered so far from our conversations, we can speculate that he would remember a place like that. He likes solitude and quietness and that place has all of that and more. He could stay there for weeks and no one would be any the wiser. The entrance to the dirt road is all but hidden by brush and overgrown weeds. And that was years ago. I can only imagine what it must look like now."

As he told her the details, Chris became more and more convinced that he may be on to something. It was close and hidden from view. They knew that Kevin hadn't gone past the roadblocks and yet he hadn't surfaced anywhere in a week. Logically, it made perfect sense. She couldn't keep her heart from pounding in anticipation.

"Brad, we have to call the police and tell them about what you are thinking. They can go there and check it out."

"No. I will not send them in there without knowing where they are going. I know all the roads that lead there like the back of my hand. I grew up going there to fish and hunt in the summers. If the police charge in there with sirens blazing Rick may feel cornered and do something rash. I need to do this."

She saw the determination in his face and didn't argue. The only question was when would he be able to go? Time was ticking and he could decide to move on at any time. Brad gingerly lifted himself off the bed and tried to stand. He was so tired but now he had a plan and he needed to get his strength back quickly.

He must be as crazy as his brother was. He was in no shape to be playing Chuck Norris. He had acted brave and in control while Chris was here, but now he was worried. What if he messed up and caused Ashley or Katie to be killed? On the off chance that they were hiding out in the cabin, how would he get them out? Maybe they should just call the police.

The food service lady entered his room with his dinner tray and for the first time in days he ate heartily. He was going to need to get his energy back as soon as possible if he was going to pull this off. Rick had proven himself to be violent and impulsive, but he was very intelligent. He must have an excellent memory as well. Brad himself couldn't even remember what all he had told Rick when he thought he wasn't going to make it, but apparently Rick remembered every clue. He had came here and singled out Ashley. Then he had won her heart and built her the house of her dreams using everything Brad had told him about her. Would he have taken her to the cabin? It made perfect sense to him.

Ashley

She could feel the change in Kevin when she awoke that morning. He was tense and antsy and snapped at her for everything she did. He kept them inside the house and kept watching out the windows. He paced the floor and yelled at Katie for playing. By the time lunch time arrived, her nerves were frazzled and she really needed a break from the tension.

"Kevin, why don't we all go for a walk? I, for one, could use some fresh air. What about it?"

He took his time in answering. She had almost decided that he hadn't heard her when he finally turned from the window and nodded. She couldn't believe he had agreed. She quickly packed some lunch items and out the door they went. She kept one ear open for the sound of engines and one eye on the sky. Surely the police were using planes to search for them, but she had, as of yet, to see one.

They walked down to the river and continued up an overgrown trail. At one point the trail went around the edge of a rocky hill and Ashley eyed the river far below them. She fantasized about suddenly giving him a hard shove and him falling over the edge. As if reading her mind, Kevin reached out and grabbed a hold of Katie's ponytail and eyed Ashley warily.

"Go ahead and push me. I'm taking her with me. As a matter of fact, maybe I'll just do you a favor and jump." Katie looked down and yelled out in fear. Ashley almost fainted at the idea of Katie falling into the river below.

"Stop, Kevin! Please be careful." She reached out to grab Katie's hand to help her back onto the trail. Ashley didn't breathe until they had again reached level ground.

Would he have really hurt Katie? Of course he would have. This thought haunted her all the way. What kind of monster would hurt a little girl? She knew that there were bad people in the world, but it still amazed her that she lived with this one. She wondered if there was another way back that would avoid going over that steep path. She didn't think she could trust him again. What if he went off and just shoved her or Katie over the edge?

It would be easier on him if they were dead. He could just slip away and change identities again. The only thing keeping them alive at this point was his deranged idea that she belonged to him and loved him. She must under all circumstances keep him believing that she needed him. His sense of self-worth was making him feel confident of their escape.

They came to an opening in the woods that took her breath away. The woods here were clear and unblemished with last autumn's leaves and needles quietly blanketing the forest floor. The sun rays slanted through the pine boughs creating an almost dreamlike effect. Kevin even seemed taken aback by the beauty here. Katie danced and ran around the soft earthen floor with Rosie chasing her all the way. Ashley sat down on a log and watched Kevin. He had his hands on his hips and was watching Katie play. She knew within her heart that somewhere inside of him he loved her. She had seen too much in the beginning to contradict it. No one could be that skilled of an actor. He had loved Katie like she was his daughter. She still cringed at the thought that he had secretly filed adoption papers while she had been sedated. Surely that legal decision would be overruled when he was caught.

How was it possible that a person could change so drastically or be so conniving? She studied his face in profile and remembered when she had loved him so deeply. She remembered when she had gazed into his eyes in wonder at the love she felt. Now she just felt empty when she studied him. She felt remorseful and hurt and bitter. Anger was a slightly new emotion for her to experience. Yes, she had been bewildered when Brad left, but she hadn't felt anger of this magnitude before. She wanted her life to be normal again.

She wanted to go back to that day at the restaurant when she had met Kevin. Of course, knowing what she knew now, she realized that Kevin had been looking for her and he would have found her wherever she had been. This was an eerie feeling, kind of like predator and prey. Silently, she shook herself.

She called Katie to come and eat and began to get out lunch. She noticed that her hands were shaking. There had to be some end to the nonsense. After eating, Katie took off again to run and play. Ashley carefully wrapped up the leftovers and turned to where Kevin was sitting.

"Kevin, I need to talk to you."

"What is it, Ashley? I could tell that you were deep in thought earlier and wondered when you would come to me."

He got up and moved to sit behind her and put his arms around her. He let his head drop down on her shoulder and she cringed when he kissed her neck.

"Kevin, I have started to rethink our decision to move. Do you think there is any way possible that we could stay? Katie is in school and I hate for her to have to start somewhere new. We've just now got our house completed and I love it. It is all I have dreamed of. You are all I have dreamed of." She braced herself for the explosion she knew was coming.

"Ashley, don't be afraid to come to me with your fears and worries. You know that I only want to make you happy. Why didn't you tell me you didn't want to move?"

She held perfectly still lest the spell be broken. She didn't even breathe. What was he doing? He had taken her against her will and now he was acting like it was her decision to stay.

"What do you mean, Kevin?"

"I mean that if you don't want to go, we won't go. We will go back home and deal with our problems. You will go to trial for killing Sandra. I will go to trial for hurting Chris and Daniel and now Brad. We will both do our time in jail and then we will live happily ever after. I'll be honest with you, honey. I don't want to go back to jail. I've done my time there and it isn't like on TV. But if that is what you really want to do, I'll do it. I love you that much. Of course, they will take Katie away. They don't like kids to raise themselves while their parents are in the pen. I am sure we can all catch up when we get out in say, ten, fifteen years."

She turned and looked at him in disbelief. At her stunned look, he burst out laughing. "Just kidding, honey. Don't look so scared. I would never do that to you. I am getting you away from that chaos. I know that you were joking about not wanting to move. Of course you know the consequences of all that has happened and the only option is for us to move on."
The confusion she had felt seconds ago gave way to disappointment. How could she have thought he was serious? He was crazy. He would never let her go.

Chris

She had been driving around in circles for most of the afternoon. Somewhere out here her sister was being held and she didn't know what else to do except to just look around. She thought that she knew most of the roads in the county, but as she drove she noticed several overgrown old roads that she hadn't known existed. There were a lot of abandoned and dilapidated houses too. She drove up to each one and got out to check them out. She looked for any sign that Ashley had been there. She went to the local campground and even went so far as to go through the garbage. She knew that she was acting like a desperate fool but she needed to be busy. She couldn't just sit at home and mope around wondering what happened. Surely, Ashley would figure out a way to call her or contact her some way. The fact that she hadn't yet only made Chris extremely nervous. Either she didn't have access to a phone or she was unable to call. Chris could hardly even think of the latter option. She wouldn't allow herself to go down that alley. She had to keep positive and eventually someone would find a clue that would lead them to Ashley and Katie.

Brad had been very secretive about where he suspected they might be and it infuriated her to no end that he wouldn't share with her. She could have already notified the police and known for sure if they were there, but he was adamant about going himself. He was scheduled to leave the hospital tomorrow and she would be sure to be there when he left the hospital. He wouldn't know it, but she would see him safely home. There was no way she was letting him go there alone in the shape he was in. What if, God forbid, he found them? Kevin would probably kill him on the spot and then no one would ever find a trace of where he had went. Ashley and Katie would be history. She couldn't let her only lead disappear.

What day was this? She should head on home and get dinner started for her family. Carley probably had some school function and Drew probably had ball practice. She had lost track of her kids in the last few weeks. She didn't have the energy to focus on all of them at once. Maybe tomorrow would be the end of this hell.

Brad

He was out of the hospital and he had never been so relieved. He had a mission to accomplish and he felt an urgency like none he had ever felt before. This was his daughter they were talking about. As expected, Chris had arrived a little while ago to drive him home. She thought that she was going to go with him to check it out, but he had news for her. He wasn't going to go if she went with him. He couldn't risk her life, as well as his. He needed to know that someone out there would notify the police on the chance that he ran into trouble. He had remembered last night more information that validated his suspicions. He remembered a time when he and Rick had been looking through old pictures. In one of them Brad was holding up a fish he had just caught. The fish had been his pride and joy and he still remembered his excitement to this day. Rick had asked him where he had caught it and he had told him he had caught it at the old fishing cabin near his hometown. Rick had been fascinated.

Of course, he hadn't had the opportunity as a child to experience simple things like fishing and hunting. He always made Brad tell him every detail of his adventures. Now he knew that Rick had been cataloging these moments in his mind and he would remember where the cabin was.

As soon as Chris and Brad pulled into her driveway they both jumped out of the car. Brad needed some supplies. To his surprise he found a whole arsenal laid out on the dining room table. She had arranged flashlights, ropes, cell phones, and all types of gear. He couldn't help but laugh at her effort to supply him with everything he might need.

"What's so funny?" she asked in mock surprise.

"I just didn't expect you to be so prepared. Of course, I should have expected it. You always were the responsible one."

At this she gazed at him thoughtfully. "Brad, I am so worried about you. You are in no shape to go out there alone. Please let me go or call the police. They are trained and know how to handle him." He was adamant.

"No, Chris. I caused this, and I am going to go help Ashley and Katie myself. I am feeling better and better and I really feel like I will be okay. If I get in a situation I can't handle, I will use this handy cell phone here and call for help."

"Yeah, make fun now, but you will appreciate my preparations later on when you need mosquito repellant."

They both laughed and Brad began to get together what he needed. He couldn't believe she had even thought of a GPS. This woman was determined to let nothing keep him away from Ashley. A few minutes later he went out to Chris' car and got in.

"I'll call you in an hour. By then I should know if I am right and they are there or not. If for some reason I don't check in with you in one hour, go ahead and call the police. And Chris, I am not going to go charging in there ready to save the day. If I see any sign of them, I will stop and wait for the police to get there." He waved and backed out of the driveway.

Chris

She had never been so nervous. If Brad's hunch was right and Kevin had Ashley and Katie there, something was about to happen. One way or another, this should be over quickly. She went to the back of the house and got into Daniel's old Jeep. It hadn't been driven in several months and was hard to crank. Finally, after several attempts, she heard a satisfying roar.

"Come on, old gal. Let's see if you have any life left in you." She coaxed the manual transmission into first gear and slowly let out the clutch. With a sudden lurch, she was in motion. She yelled in relief and accelerated down the driveway. She had driven about a quarter mile when she saw Brad in the distance up ahead. Slowly she dropped behind just far enough for him not to recognize her. She was going to follow him as far as she could by vehicle, and then she would run if she had to. She was going to be there when Ashley was found. She knew deep in her heart that Brad's idea was right and they would be there.

Ashley

It had been a long day and she was very tired. They had trekked back through the woods towards the cabin without anyone talking. She wondered how much farther it could be to the stupid cabin. Kevin had lead them on this little adventure and she really had no idea where they were. Another hour passed and Ashley felt sorry for Katie. She knew that her little legs had to be sore and tired. They had been walking for what seemed like hours. She looked up at the sun and guessed it was probably around three o'clock.

Katie's shoulders were sunburned too, and this made Ashley mad. She looked up at Kevin's back and wished she had her gun back. Damn it, she wanted to leave! She wanted to go home and take a shower and tuck Katie into her soft bed and kiss her goodnight. Katie was a tough little kid but she could only take so much. Ashley gently reached out and tugged on a pigtail. When Katie turned around Ashley held out her arms and offered to carry her. Katie willingly climbed up on her mom's back to ride. Kevin turned around and looked at them in distain.

"Sissy little girl. Neither one of you have any endurance. Maybe when we get out west we will put you both in a boot camp to toughen you up."

He seemed to find this extremely funny. Ashley wasn't impressed at all. Out West? Is that where he thought he was going to take her?

"Yeah, honey. I think tonight is the night, don't you? I'll bet the search for you and Katie has been called off. Actually I know it has been, because I listened to the radio in the car this morning. Yep, called off the search. Shouldn't be too hard to get out of here and head out west. The town I am thinking of shouldn't have many nosy neighbors. Nice and quiet. Just you and me and Katie."

Ashley felt the solid weight on her back and knew that Katie had fallen asleep.

"Kevin, I am not going to go with you. You are a madman and need mental help. I am going to divorce you and I really hope to never see your ugly face again."

Ashley stopped in her tracks. Had she said that out loud? Leaves crunched as Kevin stopped also and slowly turned around to face her. He was breathing hard and his eyes were dangerous. Sweat ran down her back and over her brow.

"Did you say something dear? I heard you mumbling but I couldn't understand you." She released her pent up breath and smiled sweetly.

"Just singing a song, honey. I'm sorry." She waited while he decided what to do next. Finally, he turned back around and continued on his way. Ashley was left with no choice but to follow. Stupid! He couldn't know how she felt. He would kill her and Katie. She would have to be more careful.

Tonight, he had said. She wracked her brain trying to come up with a plan of escape. Maybe she could just take off running and hope he couldn't catch her. Yeah, right. She instantly dismissed this idea as suicide. He would catch her in less than twenty feet. Maybe she could somehow get the keys to the car and race away. No. He had the keys in his pocket and watched her continuously. She couldn't very well wrestle him and win either, even though she had dreamed of this often. Could she stab him with a knife? Chances are that it wouldn't injure him or kill him immediately and he would retaliate. Maybe . . . . They reached the road. Was this the same one that they had taken on the way in? Regardless, it was easier to walk without all the briars and broken down trees to dodge. She was tired and Katie was getting heavier by the minute.

Without any warning, Kevin turned around and slapped her across the face. The force of the blow knocked her off of her feet and Katie went sprawling. Katie immediately began screeching in pain and fear after being awakened so brutally. Her hair was full of leaves and she had landed on the gravel and cut her forehead and elbow. Ashley staggered over to where she was and gathered her into her arms.

"Leave her alone. She needs to toughen up. Get up!" Kevin shouted. Ashley looked at him in disbelief. He really thought that she would leave Katie lying here crying in the dirt?

"Did you hear me, Ashley? You are a no-good mother and a no-good wife. You don't deserve to have a husband like me who puts up with your selfishness. Babying Katie isn't doing her any good. I said to get up and let her cry. I didn't have my mom petting me whenever I fell down."

Ashley just stared at him and shook her head. Oh Lord, he had gone even crazier. He crossed to where they were sitting and grabbed Ashley by the hair. He jerked her up so violently that she screamed. Tears poured down her face from the pain, not just physical but the pain of hearing Katie screaming in fear.

Katie

The bad Kevin was back and Katie was so scared. Mommy was yelling and trying to get away from him, but he had a hold of her hair and she couldn't make him let go. One minute she had been sleeping and then next she was crashing to the ground. Confused and bewildered she ran up to Kevin and bit him on the leg as hard as she could. He yelped and slapped her in the top of the head but at least he had loosened his grip on Mom long enough for her to back away. Mom yelled at her to run to her as fast as she could and she did. She was a fast runner, all the kids at school said so. When she reached Mom, she grabbed her hand.

"Katie, run away. Run as fast as you can and do not turn back. Find somewhere safe to hide until you see help coming. Hide! Do not come out for anything. Stay there!"

Kevin reached them in a few easy strides and grabbed Mom around the waist and threw her down on the ground. He hit her over and over again and Katie knew it when her Mom went to sleep. Kevin was huffing and puffing and yelling. She had never seen anyone so angry. Next, he picked up a giant rock and was leaning back to hit Mom in the head with it. Katie cringed and cried out.

Then, from out of nowhere, Rosie leapt. All of the hair on her back was sticking up and her ears were laid back against her neck. She seemed to fly through the air. Katie could see her big teeth shining and if she hadn't known it was Rosie she would have been scared. Katie ran backwards and watched as if in slow motion as Rosie sank her teeth deeply into the flesh of Kevin's neck. The rock fell to the side, forgotten in his pain. Katie couldn't wait any longer, for she feared that Kevin would kill her next. She ran and ran on the road. She ran when her side hurt so badly that she cried. She ran even when she couldn't breathe anymore. Finally, she collapsed on the dirt and lay down. The rocks were sharp on her back and the sticks poked through her shirt, but she didn't care. Her mommy was probably up in heaven now and Katie was alone. Kevin had probably killed Rosie as well. She buried her face in her dirty hands and wept.

Brad

He had found the entryway easy enough. Now to see if Chris' car would make it down the washed out and pitted road. He would just go as far as possible by car, and then he would walk the rest of the way. Right away he could see evidence that another vehicle had been down here. Some of the dried grass and weeds were broken. Now to go see who had ventured here. The bottom of the car scrapped and scraped over the ruts and he winced. Daniel would kill him when he saw this. As far as he knew, Daniel didn't even know about this little excursion. He had spent his last several days searching for a job and today he had had an interview. Maybe all of this would be over by the time he got home and asked about the car.

If he found Ashley and Katie and they were okay, then maybe a little damage to a car would seem insubstantial. About three quarters of a mile into the woods he decided that this was as far as he could venture with the car. He stopped and put the car in reverse. He planned to back the car into a little natural opening in the woods and walk in the rest of the way.

He had only taken about fifteen steps when he stopped cold in his tracks. He felt all the blood in his body drain down to his feet. Lying right in the middle of the overgrown road was a little girl. She could only be Katie. Her head was turned away from him but he knew that hair color. He had seen that hair everyday of his life in his own mirror. It must have only been a second but it felt like it took him an eternity to reach her.

As if in a dream he saw himself running and bending to touch his daughter with fear. He was shocked to see that she was breathing and she rustled slightly when he touched her. He scooped her up and held her close. Her poor body had taken quite a beating. Seemed like there was at least a little bit of blood everywhere that his eyes caressed. He had almost made it back to the car when he heard the sound of footsteps. Completely unable to protect himself or Katie in this position with her in his arms, he immediately went into a crouch and hid in a bush. His heart pounding so loudly that he could barely make out the sound. If Rick had a gun, it was all over now.

Relief and anger washed over him when he saw Chris striding down the road as if going on a Sunday stroll. He saw her hesitate and glance around when she saw the empty car and then she continued with more caution. Suddenly, he stood from his hiding spot and couldn't repress a second of gratification when she jumped in fear. They met in unison with Katie held between them.

"Is she?" Chris couldn't finish her sentence. Brad shook his head and gently transferred Katie to her aunt's awaiting arms.

"Go, Chris. Take her in your car and go back. Call the police." Brad didn't feel the need to explain that if Katie was lying here alone then obviously Ashley was in grave danger.

Misty Erwin

Chris

She didn't hesitate to even think about the fate of her sister right now. She only knew that Brad needed help and he needed it now. She should have called the police before. She placed Katie in the backseat of her car and dialed 911. There wasn't very good reception here and she couldn't be sure that the lady had heard the directions. She put the car in drive and drove as fast as she safely could. After a few minutes of being jostled, Katie sat up and looked around. Chris turned to look over her shoulder at her little niece.

"Is Mommy in heaven?" Katie asked quietly.

"Katie, what happened? Where is your mother?"

"I don't know, Aunt Chris. I ran away just like she told me to. The bad Kevin came back and he was being so mean. He hit me and Mommy and Rosie bit him. Then I ran as fast as I could."

Chris shuddered at the scene Katie described. She honestly didn't know if Ashley would have survived this long. She could only hope and pray that help reached her in time.

Katie

She had only done as Mommy had asked. Now she felt bad because she had left Mommy. Kevin probably had hurt her even worse after she had run away. Now she was to blame for Mommy getting hurt. She should have bit him again. Aunt Chris had told her that she was being silly, that of course she couldn't have protected her Mom from someone like Kevin. But Katie wondered. She tugged at her short-sleeved shirt and tried to forget about the chill in the air.

Chris had pulled over on the side of the dirt road because some police cars were coming. Katie was supposed to wait in the car for Chris to talk to them.

She had to go back. She took one more look up at the police cars with the shining lights and loud sirens and then she turned away. She and Mommy were in this together.

Brad

Just a little bit further and he should be able to see the cabin around the bend. He crept up to a large oak tree and peered around it in the direction of the hideout. A flash of color caught his attention and he focused in on that direction. One step at a time, he went forward until he had a better view. Up ahead was Rick. He was loading something into the trunk of the car. Brad moved a few more feet closer for a better look. Rick momentarily disappeared from view as he bent down on the other side of the car. Brad took this opportunity to move in as close as was safe. He could hear sounds coming from Rick's direction but he couldn't see what he was doing and he couldn't find any sign of Ashley. He darted behind a large tree when Rick suddenly appeared behind the car.

What was he doing back there? Moving with determination, Rick walked over to the driver's side of the car and got in. He started the engine and gunned it, throwing dirt and rocks several feet behind the car. Brad only got a glimpse inside the car but he didn't see anything that resembled a passenger. He dove into the brush on the side of the road to avoid being seen. He couldn't be sure that Ashley had been with him. Brad heaved a sigh of relief because he was sure that Rick would run right into the police on his way out. They had had plenty of time to get here and probably had the entire area covered. For once he was glad that there was only one road into this place and that meant only one way out. Please let Ashley be okay. He really had so much he needed to tell her.

As lost in thought as he had been, Brad had failed to hear the approaching footsteps behind him until they were only a few feet away. He spun around and instinctively braced himself for attack with both arms up. He was no match for Rick as he came barreling towards him and hit him directly in the stomach with a large limb. Brad doubled over in agony and braced himself as best as he could for the next blow. Rick placed the hit with deadly accuracy and the gunshot wound that had begun healing was once again bleeding profusely. He could feel it running in warm streams down his ribs and feared that he would lose consciousness. Somewhere in all the confusion he heard the sound of Ashley's voice pleading with Rick.

"I'll go with you, Kevin, just please don't kill Brad. Please. I'll do anything you want me to."

Ashley

She wasn't able to sit up but she could see what was going on. Kevin was killing Brad right before her eyes. There was so much blood on the front of Brad's shirt that she couldn't tell what color it originally had been. She pulled herself up on her hands and steadied herself. She yelled at Kevin and pleaded with him. She promised him anything she could think of to get him to stop hitting Brad. She felt each blow that Brad absorbed from deep in her heart. She saw the pained look on his face and she felt his anguish.

Even though the two brothers were a distance from her, she felt like Brad saw her and gave her a look of gratitude. She wondered if he would make it out of here alive.

Obviously he had come here looking for her and Katie. Katie. Oh, dear Lord, where was her Katie? She didn't think she could bear the pain that came with thinking about Katie. She had run just like Ashley had told her to. Now Ashley didn't know where she was or if she was okay. It was a long way out this old road and who knew the hazards Katie might face trying to go get help. Ashley silently prayed for God to send Rosie to find Katie and help her. She hadn't seen Rosie since hours before when she had bitten Kevin. He had hit her and she had run off yelping. She may be dead for all Ashley knew.

Out of the corner of her eye, Ashley saw a glimpse of pink through the trees behind Kevin and Brad. She sat up suddenly and had to fight a wave of dizziness. She forced her eyes to focus on the exact spot where she had seen movement. Nothing. Maybe she was just delirious. Dusk was setting and it made it hard to differentiate between colors. With all the blows to the head she had taken, it would be no wonder if she had a fractured skull.

Again. Down at the cabin Ashley saw a flash of movement but she couldn't follow it because Kevin and Brad were between her and the cabin. Instinctually, she got out of the car and started trying to walk. Shock stopped her in her tracks. Coming from the cabin was a thin line of smoke. Or was that her imagination? Katie? No, that was definitely smoke and it was getting thicker by the moment. She saw the front door of the cabin swing shut and that's when she knew that Katie had come back. Katie had come back and she was in the cabin which was on fire. She began to jog and then to run. She tripped over fallen limbs and debris but she just got back up and ran again. She distantly heard Kevin shouting at her but she didn't even slow down. She had one focus. She had to get to her daughter.

Brad

This was the end. He wasn't even as scared as he had thought he would be. He didn't even feel any pain any more. Rick had stopped punching and kicking him and was chasing after Ashley. Brad lay face down on the forest floor and smelled the pungent aroma of pine needles and decaying leaves. It was so comfortable here. He would just lie here a minute and go to sleep. A shiny object amid all the leaves caught his attention, just as he drifted off. He opened one eye and tried to see what it was. The barrel of a pistol? That wasn't possible. The only things he had with him were in the backpack Chris had made for him. Chris. He sat up and rubbed his eyes. She would have packed a pistol. He gingerly reached out and rubbed the grips as if afraid it would vanish into thin air. When he realized it wasn't a dream he gripped the pistol and tried to stand. Ashley was screaming for Katie. He had to go help Katie, if it was the last thing he did.

Something was badly wrong for Ashley to be screaming that way. He rose up on his hands and knees and saw the object of Ashley's terror. The cabin was on fire. The entire south side was engulfed in flames and they were creeping along the front wall.

Brad somehow found the strength to run and he followed Rick and Ashley down the hill towards the inferno. He heard the precious sound of sirens approaching from a distance.

Rick

This woman couldn't be stopped. Every time he thought she had decided to submit to him and behave, she did something stupid like this. Like right now she was running right back towards the cabin they had just left. Didn't she see that the stupid place was on fire? He had decided to erase all evidence they might have left behind. She was screaming for Katie. Maybe she had completely lost her mind. They had both seen Katie running in the opposite direction hours earlier. He had seen signs of her mental disorder in the past but this took the cake.

And so what if Katie had stupidly returned here? She was just a kid and they could have more of them whenever they got settled into their new place. Kids were nothing but trouble, as far as he could see. She was always into something and then she had become defiant and that was something he couldn't abide by. No, even if she had not ran away he would have probably had to end her. He had tried and tried to break her but she had her mother's tenaciousness. Probably better for her to be killed like this anyway. That way Ashley wouldn't always blame him for her death.

He pushed a little bit harder and jumped on top of Ashley as she ran. She went sprawling, flat down on her face with him on top of her.

"You bastard! Get off of me!" She struggled to crawl out from under him but he was so much bigger than her. He pinned her down and yelled at her.

"Ashley get a hold of yourself. Stop fighting me!"

Chris

How could a five year old little girl simply walk away from her and several policemen and none of them see her? She felt so useless and disappointing. Her only job in this had been to get Katie out of here and to safety and she obviously couldn't even do that right. Where had she gone? She hoped that if she was looking for Rosie that she didn't find her dead. Katie had been through enough without seeing her pet laying dead in the woods. She was sure that Kevin had killed her.

Chris absently wiped the sweat from her brow with the back of her hand. She had run around and around yelling for Katie and now she was having a severe case of de ja vu. Seemed like not long ago that everyone had been doing the same thing. Whenever she found the little devil she would get a piece of Chris' mind. It had been long moments ago when three police vehicles had flown by Chris' parked car with siren screaming. If Kevin hadn't already known his hideout was not a secret anymore, then now he certainly did. Please Lord, let Ashley be alive and hang in there until help arrived.

Brad

He staggered towards Rick with the pistol in his hand. Rick had Ashley pinned down underneath him and she was fighting him savagely. Someone had to go get Katie from the cabin. Brad struggled to think clearly through the pain and the blood loss. Should he go help Ashley or Katie? Where were the damn cops? He needed help and he needed it now.

It seemed like time crawled. Rick must have heard him approaching because he turned and looked over his shoulder at him.

"You just won't die will you? How many times have I tried to get you people off my back? Ashley and I just want to leave here peacefully and start our new lives together."

With this he backhanded Ashley and she stopped struggling. Brad slowly raised the pistol and pointed it at Rick.

"What? You going to kill me? I'm your brother, man. We are flesh and blood and nothing can come between us. Please help me get out of here, Brad. I need your help."

"I need you to get down on your stomach on the ground and stay there until police get here. Katie needs help now and I am going to go get her out." Brad gestured with the gun for Kevin to lie down.

"Lie down? What, just like our mother did? That is the coward's way out. I won't go with the police again Brad. They will have to kill me. I won't go down without a fight."

Brad couldn't help but hesitate at the mention of his mother. "My mother was not even in the same class as you, Rick. She was a good, hard-working woman who somehow got involved with your no-good father. When he finally died, she did what she knew was best and left you. She knew even then that you would turn out just like your sorry father."

"Oh, yeah. Well, I got my revenge didn't I? I didn't deserve to be left with my selfish aunt for the simple reason that I had been born. Do you know what kind of childhood I had? While you and all your blessed siblings lived the good life in a nice house and plenty of food and clothes, I was starving and neglected. Your mother didn't deserve to die as easy as she did. I should have made it even harder. She should have suffered more."

Brad couldn't believe what he was hearing. Had this man just admitted to killing his mother? Brad tried to think back to when she had been so sick and to connect it to Rick in any way and he came up short.

"What do you mean? What did you have to do with Mom's death?"

Rick threw back his head and laughed. "You think she just passed away from natural causes after living a wonderful life of giving generously to the poor? No, dear brother, she did not. I only wish she could have suffered a lot longer."

Brad lost control and lunged at Rick. The brothers fought for a few seconds and the pistol was fired.

Rick collapsed onto the dirt and didn't move again. Brad fought for control of his anger. He was breathing so hard that his chest hurt. He fell back onto his back and looked up at the sky. He had killed Mom? The smell of smoke broke through his pain and Brad turned over and looked again at the cabin. He had to get to Katie before it was too late and he didn't honestly know how he was going to get all the way over there in the shape he was in. With all the strength he had left he crawled towards the cabin.

Ashley

Through the fog she struggled back towards awareness. Katie was in the cabin and it was on fire. She rolled onto her stomach and rose up on all fours. She lifted her head and saw Brad struggling to crawl towards the cabin. Kevin was nowhere to be seen. She glanced suspiciously around her, expecting him to be behind her, ready to finish her off. Relief overwhelmed her when she didn't see him and she stood up and began to run. The cabin was not that far away, yet it seemed like miles. It seemed like hours had passed since she had realized that Katie was inside. Could she still be alive in there with all the smoke and heat?

Oh Dear Lord, please save my baby, she sobbed. She finally reached the front door and was thoroughly shocked when she tried to turn the knob and it was locked. Panic crashed through her and she screamed and banged on the door. Suddenly an entire squad of police and rescue vehicles entered the little clearing. She ran towards them yelling for help. She told the first man she saw that her daughter was trapped in the cabin and then she ran back towards the back door. Through her tears she saw movement ahead. She saw first her tail and then her back. Rosie was pulling Katie from the burning cabin.

Katie

So I waited. I waited until the temperature of the air dropped and I shivered. I waited until the light diminished and I couldn't see my own hand trembling. I waited when I heard a steady knock on the door. Even when they called my name I waited.

Some people still ask me why I didn't answer. The answer is that I don't know. I was unable to respond, I guess. The smell of smoke burned my lungs and the sound of the sirens lured me into myself. I was as quiet as a mouse. Just as she asked me to be. I was a good little girl.

Epilogue

It is a quiet life. Some people don't understand the magnificent pull of the force that beckons people here. I understand. It is safe here, away from the turmoil. It is far better to know what is ahead than to think of what is behind you. Here, you don't ever think of the past, you dream of the future. An often-viewed, folded piece of paper falls from my journal as I shift on my cot. Once again I read the newspaper article that I have memorized. With resolution, I tuck it back away.

I hear the sweet sound of her voice drifting outside my little window and smile. I turn back to my writing.

> *Sometimes I wonder why butterflies seem to fly in zig zags. Their flight seems so uncharted and undecided and yet they always find a flower. And when they light on the soft petals they seem so content and calm and peaceful. They seem to not recall the confusion from a few moments before. I wonder if that is the way people live their lives. We wonder around aimlessly and confused all the while knowing exactly what we are looking for but not sure of the path it will take to get there. Even when we know what we need, we are wrong in the way we seek it. If only we could just get to our eternity. Then we could look back and laugh at the mistakes we made before, and consume the sweet nectar of never land.*

I sigh contently and fixed my eyes on the crucifix hanging above my bed. I have been journaling ever since the day I came here to live and that seems to help. Even though I am safe here with the sisters, I shudder when the thoughts cross my mind, uninvited. He is still out there somewhere. And a tear runs down my cheek.